DELAYED GAME

BAYLIN CROW

Delayed Game by Baylin Crow

Copyright 2021 Baylin Crow

This is a work of fiction. All characters, locations and events portrayed in this work are either fictitious or are used fictitiously. Any similarity is purely coincidental.

The use of any real company and/or product names is for literary effect only. All other trademarks and copyrights are the property of their respective owners.

All rights reserved.

No part of this publication may be reproduced in any written, electronic, recording or photocopying without written permission from the publisher or author. The exception would be in the case of brief quotations embodied in the critical articles or reviews and pages where permission is specifically granted by the publisher or author.

Any images or models shown on covers are for illustration purposes only. The characters depicted and any texts expressed in this story are not reflective of any models shown.

Edited by Jamie Piatt

Proofread by Kathy Kozakewich

Cover Design by Cate Ashwood

 Created with Vellum

SERIES NOTE

While there is a real Sugar Land, Texas, the fictional city this book takes place in is simply that. Fictional. Each story in the Sugar Land Saints Series will be semi-standalone and each will focus on a new couple. You can read them separately, but I recommend reading them in order. Characters from previous books in the series will make appearances and be referenced.

Hope you enjoy!

Baylin xo

ONE

TRISTAN

THE BELL RANG, and chairs scraped across the shiny linoleum floor of Parksville High School as everyone stood to leave. Sliding out from my desk, I grabbed my backpack from the floor and stuffed my Trigonometry book inside.

Mr. Dunham cleared his throat, trying to regain our attention. He stood next to the projector that displayed a complicated problem on a white screen in the darkened room. "There will be a test on Monday. Review your materials and come prepared," he reminded us.

No one acknowledged him, but I nodded as I waited until most of the students cleared the room before heading for the door. Nudging my way into the crowded hallway, I squeezed between a girl who was embarrassingly taller than me, and a clumsy oaf that played on our varsity football team. I wiggled free and barely dodged an elbow to the chest for my efforts.

The halls echoed with a constant buzz of laughter, lockers slamming shut, and exciting conversations about the quickly approaching summer. I tuned it all out as I slid in front of my locker and switched my books out for my next class. I still had one more period to get through before school let out for the day, and then, only one more week before I'd be out of this place for good.

A jarring thud hit the locker next to mine, startling me. I jerked my gaze up and met a pair of russet-brown eyes set in a chiseled face framed by waves of light locks. The same face I'd foolishly crushed on for all four years of high school stared back at me.

Brantley O'Brien, the baseball team's star pitcher, flashed a blinding grin full of stupidly perfect white teeth. "The boys are throwing another party tonight at Anderson's house." He bit his lip as he eyed me in a way that would have made my cock jerk before last weekend. Hooded eyes dipped to my lips before making a slow crawl up to meeting mine again. "You should come."

I lifted one brow. "Uh... why would I want to come to one of your jock-infested parties?"

"With the guys distracted, we could have a little fun." He suggestively bit his lip, and I held back an eye roll.

Looking back at my overstuffed backpack, I tugged the zipper closed. "Thought you said no repeats."

Brantley was an asshole, but he was skilled at thickly laying on the charm when he wanted to. I wasn't blind, though. I knew what it was—fake as fuck because he wanted to get in my pants. Or, instead, my mouth, most likely. Again.

He was also firmly in the closet. Then again, so was I, so I couldn't hold it against him. Not that gender ever slowed him down. If the rumors were true, Brantley had hooked up with half of the girls at school. As a premier baseball player with a full ride to college, he had his pick of girls and had used that fact to his full advantage for as long as I'd known him.

By *known*, I meant since I'd watched him with a constant hard-on in my pants while he'd barely acknowledged me, until recently.

As of last weekend, my dumb ass had added my name to the notches on his bedpost. Sort of. Drunk at a party, I'd blown him in a bathroom. He hadn't even kissed me, much less returned the favor. *Dick.*

I'd known he was an asshole, but in my defense, I'd come to terms with being gay years earlier but had never touched a guy before. With my libido set on desperate, it had only taken a few beers and an hour of his attention focused on me before I'd dropped to my knees and had his cock in my mouth. It had to have been the worst blow job of his life, but it sure hadn't stopped him from coming like a geyser. So, I'd blown a guy but still hadn't kissed one.

Classy, Tristan. I immediately squashed that self-deprecating train of thought. Slut-shaming wasn't my thing, so I'd be damned if I did it to myself.

"So?" Brantley asked, and I flicked my gaze back to him. With his eyes blazing a trail of unwelcome heat through my clothes, he lowered his voice. "Maybe I changed my mind. We had fun, right?"

Fun wasn't the word I'd use since he'd bounced and left me there the second he'd finished. I wasn't sure how Brantley had known I was gay, but he'd flirted with me when no one was looking, and like an idiot, I'd lapped up the attention like the desperate virgin I was.

"I have homework," I lied as I slung my backpack over my shoulder.

After glancing around to make sure no one was lurking nearby, he leaned down closer to my face. "You have all weekend to do homework. Tristan, I really need—"

"Your dick in my mouth?" I supplied, not bothering to suppress rolling my eyes this time.

His eyelids were heavy, half-mast. "That is exactly what I had in mind. You liked it, right?"

I wasn't sure if I'd liked it or not. I mean, at the time, sure. But afterward, when Brantley had zipped up and left me on my knees? I snorted at the memory. "Pass."

The egotistical jock's eyebrows shot up. "You kidding me?"

Cocky and vain. I scolded myself again for hooking up with someone like Brantley. "Like I said, I have homework."

"Tomorrow then." His tone held an edge of command that bristled every nerve in my body.

I spoke through clenched teeth. "You'll need to find someone else to suck your dick. I'm late for class."

His jaw worked back and forth as he ground his molars. It seemed I'd bruised his fragile ego. But why the hell did he think I'd be eager for a repeat performance? I'd bet my left nut he hadn't noticed I'd even left the party shortly afterward. Finished with the conversation, I shut my locker and side-stepped him. As I tried to go around him, Brantley gripped my arm tighter than necessary and leaned down to my ear. "You're really not interested anymore, or are you just pissed you didn't get off too?"

I jerked my arm back. "I wouldn't touch your cock again with a gloved hand, much less my mouth."

He took a step back, rolling his shoulders. "You better not breathe a word about what happened."

"Don't plan to," I replied calmly. I wasn't sure why the hell he thought I'd brag about something as dumb as sucking him off, especially when I wasn't ready to tell anyone I was gay.

This time when I stepped around him, he let me pass

without issue. I made my way to my history class and took my regular seat at the back of the room. More rattled than I wanted to admit, I swiped my black hair from my forehead and took a stuttering breath as I settled in and reached for my backpack.

"All right." My teacher entered the room, tossing his tweed jacket over the back of his chair, and spoke over the noise. "Settle down."

My phone buzzed, and I discreetly pulled it from my pocket. My best friend's name flashed on the screen.

Todd: *Party at Anderson's. You're coming. Be ready at eight.*

Me: *Pass.*

Todd: *What? Why?*

I couldn't tell him it was because of Brantley. Even Todd wasn't aware I was gay, and he definitely didn't know I had hooked up with the idiot.

Me: *Tired*

Todd: *Since when do you turn down parties?*

He had a point. But going would only invite a headache. On the other hand, I shouldn't have to stay away only to avoid Brantley. It would be easy enough to dodge him. Besides, I'd said my piece and made it clear that I was done with him. With a sigh, I tapped out a reply.

Me: *Fine.*

I could almost picture his satisfied smile, glad to have a wingman.

Todd: *That's more like it.*

THE MUSIC WAS LOUD, and my vision was slightly blurred. That last beer had been a bad call, tipping the drunk scale well past tipsy.

Todd and I sat outside where we'd claimed a wooden bench on the back porch of the upscale home in the more affluent part of town. For the last hour, we'd watched the drunken idiots, both girls and guys, doing tricks on a trampoline while making bets about the next one to do something stupid. One had already cut open an eyebrow from a hard fall.

"I have to piss," I told Todd as I held out my half-empty beer for him to babysit.

"Use the one upstairs." Todd's lips curled in disgust as he shot me a warning look behind his thick glasses. Todd had curly red hair he left untamed and wore crisp button-up shirts paired with khaki shorts, the opposite of a typical party boy. It always surprised me that he was the first to jump on a party invitation. He grimaced. "Someone got sick in the other one."

"Noted." When I pushed off the bench, my head spun, but I forced one foot in front of the other while vowing never to drink that much again. I was much smaller than Todd, who stood at just under six feet and easily weighed fifty pounds more than my scrawny ass. Consuming the same amount of alcohol hit me harder and faster.

Pushing through the crowd, I found the familiar stairs and slowly made my way to the second floor. There were three doors on the left and two on the right. All except one were closed, but steady thumping and moans echoed into the hall. I breathed a sigh of relief when I found the bathroom unoccupied. After taking care of business, I opened the door and found Brantley standing across the hall with his arms crossed. He shot me a drunken smile before stalking forward, forcing me back into the bathroom. The door clicked shut, and my heart raced as my throat tightened when he flipped the lock.

"I knew you'd change your mind," he purred and pressed me against the sink.

With my hands flat against his chest, I pushed hard, causing him to stumble back, hitting the opposite wall. He must have been drunker than I was if my skinny ass could knock him over.

I scowled. "Keep dreaming. I didn't come for you."

His reddened eyes flashed in anger. "You little prick. You know you're hard up for my cock. You dropped to your knees so fast I'm shocked you didn't shatter your boney ass."

My teeth gritted together. "Fuck you, Brantley. You're the one hard up."

He lunged, gripping me tight. "You want me to jack you off? That what it'll take for you to suck my cock again?"

"Let me go," I growled. "I'm seriously not interested."

Surprisingly, his hold loosened right before he shoved off me. "Fine."

His gaze held a glint of something I couldn't name. Whatever it was, it caused my stomach to clench with unease. I took the opening he allowed and scrambled out of the bathroom, breathing a sigh of relief when I made it to the stairs without issue.

My heart was still pounding as my shaky legs carried me down to the main floor. After I made my way back to the patio, I found Todd where I'd left him, and my legs gave out as I collapsed next to him.

"You okay?" he asked while passing my beer back.

I glanced at him and found his brow furrowed in concern. Running my fingers through my hair, I jerked my gaze away and gave a sharp nod. "Yeah. I'm cool."

Todd was quiet, and I knew he didn't believe me. His

phone went off, and I blew out a sigh of relief for the distraction. But when everyone's phone started to go off around me, an unsettling feeling sank in the pit of my stomach. Seconds later, masculine moans echoed through his phone, followed by a growled sound. The voice was indistinct, but I recognized the words and froze.

"I knew you liked cock. Suck it harder."

"What the fuck?" Todd gasped. Everyone around us quieted, and the music cut off with jarring finality. With the sudden hush, the sounds cut through the silence like a sharp knife. My heart pounded, and my cheeks flushed hot. I scanned the crowded yard, noting several people also held their phones, shadowed expressions twisted in disgust.

Slowly, I turned toward Todd, who shifted uncomfortably before shutting off his phone.

Murmurs rose around me, my name on their lips. Words filtered through the ringing in my ears. Gay. Fucking Nasty. *Disgusting.*

Though I already knew the answer, I looked at Todd. "What was that?" My voice shook as he stood, avoiding my eyes. "Todd?"

My phone's text notification sounded, and I hesitantly pulled it from my pocket. The weight of a thousand stares burned through me as I swallowed hard, praying I was wrong while knowing I wasn't. I clicked on the notification, and a video dared me to press play from an unidentified number. I didn't need to click it.

The footage had been recorded at an odd angle, only showing one part of an unidentifiable guy—his dick. There I was, on my knees, my mouth wrapped around him. I squeezed my eyes shut. The phone felt foreign in my hand, and I froze on the spot. I didn't want to open my eyes, and when I finally did, I regretted it. So many people had their eyes trained on me. Some narrowed, some wide with shock, and others full of sympathy. Those hurt the most. Even though they didn't seem to regard me with disgust, no one stepped forward to intervene or perform any kind of damage control. I scrambled to my feet.

"Todd." My voice quaked. "We need to go."

Silence met my plea, and my gaze shot to my best friend. He stood quietly, arms hanging at his side as he focused on the concrete beneath his feet.

A tremor shook my body as I whispered, "Todd?"

"You better go." His voice was barely audible, yet I heard the words loud and clear.

"You're not coming with me?" I asked nervously. I needed my best friend. There was no way I could make it through the house by myself. My cheeks burned, and nausea swirled in my stomach. "Please."

He gave a ragged breath followed by a silent shake of his head. The only thing he offered was a quiet, "There's a gate at the side of the house."

I blinked in disbelief. My best friend was abandoning me at the most humiliating time of my life. Tears threatened to fill my eyes, but I refused to let everyone see them. I angrily blinked them away.

I stared at the ground wordlessly as I ignored everyone and skirted the house, finding the wooden gate and pushing it open. The voices picked up, and I could make out my name and knew they hadn't recognized the other guy. Fucking Brantley. I wasn't even sure how he'd gotten the video. The angle made it clear it wasn't in his hand, so he'd had to set it up before he'd pulled me in the bathroom, which only made me angrier. Was I that transparent, or was he just that vain and confident that I'd do what he wanted? And I'd fed right into it.

Sticking to the shadows, I let the ache in my chest give way to silent tears once the music became a dull hum in the distance. The alcohol still circulating in my veins clouded my vision and made me stumble. Embarrassment crippled me as I turned the corner on the next street and collapsed under a giant oak tree, the bark scraping my back as I slid down onto my ass. The only light came from a dim street-lamp across the street from the yard where I'd landed.

I curled in on myself, clutching my thighs to my chest, and for the first time in my life, feeling every bit of my slight frame. Heaving breaths rushed in and out of my lungs as I fought back the sobs. I swallowed, but they lodged in my constricted throat. I wouldn't give in because those people didn't deserve it, but my shoulders shook with the effort. The pressure in my chest was too much. The tears continued, unabated, streaming down my cheeks as I quietly sank into the misery of the moment. My phone vibrated in my pocket, but I ignored it. Nothing, absolutely *nothing* good, would have been sent to me at that moment, even if it were Todd, the disloyal asshole. I couldn't believe he'd abandoned me like that.

The sound of a screen door shutting barely registered. Steps came closer, and then sizeable, scuffed tennis shoes stopped in front of me. The sounds coming from my chest stopped, and I sniffed as my embarrassment doubled.

"Sorry," I mumbled and started to stand.

A deep voice that was rich and warm came from above me. "Everything okay?" I scoffed, and he murmured, "Yeah, stupid question. Are you hurt?"

"Only my pride." He wasn't giving me room to climb to my feet, so I leaned back against the tree. "I need to get home. I'm sorry if I disturbed your family."

"You didn't. I was on my way out, but I don't live here."

I nodded and swiped a finger under my eye. My cheeks were damp, and even though I was curious about whoever stood above me, I didn't want them to see my face, most likely red and blotchy, snot running out of my nose. Gross.

"Where are you from?" I asked to distract him.

"A few towns away. Do you want me to call someone?" he asked quietly.

So much for distracting him. "No, I just need to go home."

"Where's home?" His voice was patient and comforting in an unexpected way. Somehow it was soothing to the invisible, fresh wound that pierced my pride.

I shrugged. "Just a few streets over."

"Want to talk about it?" he offered, and the offer was surprising, though I didn't guess he knew what he was asking to talk about.

Still, alcohol and the bone-deep exhaustion that was settling in loosened my lips. "I'm gay."

He went so still that anger bubbled inside me. "Don't want to talk about it now, do you?"

He breathed out a harsh breath. "It's not that."

The grass next to me crunched, and then suddenly, a sinewy body lowered beside me, carrying with it a hint of cologne that reminded me of warm earthy spices. From the corner of my eye, I noticed a muscled frame in dark mesh shorts and a t-shirt with ripped sleeves, revealing defined muscles, as he settled against the bark. He wasn't touching me, but his body heat radiated comforting warmth against my side.

The guy shifted, bending his knees as his elbows loosely hung over them. "Tell me what happened."

I tilted my head so that my hair covered my face. I didn't

want him to witness the wash of pain that would inevitably show in my eyes. "And let you think I'm gross too?"

"Because you're gay?" he guessed.

I nodded as I picked at the freshly mowed grass.

"I don't think that's gross. My night was shit too." The guy sighed. "I'll trade you. I'll tell you my story if you tell me yours. Deal?"

It would be nice to open up to someone, especially if he wasn't from around town. "Why are you here?"

"What do you mean?"

"You said you aren't from here," I reminded him.

"That's all part of my shitty story. Deal or no deal?"

Curiosity won out, and I groaned in exasperation. "Fine, you evil chicken nugget. Deal."

"Chicken..." he whispered before letting out a choked cough. "That was random. You have a thing against chicken nuggets?"

"Of course not, hence the evil part. Not regular ones. Obviously." I was tempted to sneak a peek at him but forced myself not to because I was sure my eyes were puffy and bloodshot.

"*Obviously.*" He choked on a laugh, and a tiny grin snuck up unexpectedly on my lips.

"Stop stalling," I prodded, shoving my leg against his. He pushed mine back, and my grin attempted to grow, but I squashed it. I was miserable. You weren't supposed to smile when you felt like both the world and your best friend had betrayed you. "You first."

"Fine. So, this is my boyfriend's"—he stopped to fix his words— "well, now it's my ex-boyfriend's house. Who knows what he thinks I'm doing out here. Probably thinks I'm about to start stalking him."

I tensed. "Are you a stalker?"

He chuckled, the deep timbre calming. "I'm afraid I'm not quite that exciting."

His words finally registered, and my brows shot up. "You're gay?"

He hummed. "Bi, I guess. I haven't told anyone yet. Well, I guess now *you* know."

I nodded. The fact that I hadn't looked at the guy made it easier to talk to him. "You were saying?"

He cleared his throat. "We've been dating for six-ish months. Mostly long distance because I was away at college in Florida last year. I just came back a few months ago, and I was thinking about taking our relationship public."

"What did he say?" I asked.

"All kinds of things. But basically, he thought I was crazy, and he broke up with me. Or I guess it was mutual."

I couldn't decipher his tone. The words sucked, but he didn't seem all that bummed. Blaming the alcohol that flooded my body, I chanced a quick glance his way, peripherally catching a glimpse of a sharp jaw and broad shoulders. He wore a ball cap pulled low over his forehead, and I was tempted to ask him to show me his face. Instead, I concentrated again on the blades of grass beneath my fingers. "I'm sorry. So, what's the plan now? Still going to come out?"

He was quiet for a moment. "I don't think I'm ready to do that yet. Especially now."

I nodded because I understood. I hadn't exactly had a choice, but if I had, I wouldn't have been ready yet either. "Understandable."

"Your turn," he reminded me, and I groaned.

"I was stupid enough to hook up with one of the jocks from school last weekend. He wanted a repeat, but he hadn't even kissed me and then bailed afterward. My dick and I both thought that was rude."

"Definitely," he agreed. "This guy break your heart?"

I snorted. "Not even close. But he did humiliate me."

"How so?" His voice held an edge, and my heart thumped an extra beat because he sounded a little angry for someone who didn't even know my name.

I sighed as the video, or rather part of the video replayed in my mind. "The asshole taped the whole thing. I had no idea. And when I turned him down tonight, he sent it out to the whole fucking school."

He went so still that I couldn't help but look at him once again. With his jaw tensed, the guy's molars ground so hard I wondered if he was about to chip a tooth.

"Name?" His voice was so deadly monotone that I leaned away. The action caused him to look my way, and again, I wished the lighting was better. With his face shrouded in shadow, I could barely make out his full lower lip. His cupid's bow-shaped upper lip was beautifully masculine, and that strong jaw was so chiseled it appeared to be cut from granite. "You don't need to be scared of me," he whispered.

Because I knew him so well? Stupid alcohol decided the words were reassuring anyway. "You're not from here, so you wouldn't know him."

He looked away, and his breathing came harder. "Whether you tell me or not, I'll find out."

"And beat him up?" The idea held appeal, but he'd been so kind, I didn't want him to get in trouble because of a stupid decision I'd made. He hesitated long enough that I was sure the idea had tempted him too. I shook my head. "I'm not letting you do that."

He huffed. "No, I won't beat him up. But I wouldn't be mad if it happened to him."

Why did he seem to care so much about someone he'd just met?

"Me neither." I stood slowly and brushed the dirt off my pants. "That's enough of my sob story. Thanks for listening, and I'm sorry your boyfriend did that to you. If it helps, I wouldn't mind if someone kicked his ass too."

He glanced up, and though I couldn't see his eyes, a dimple popped as he gave me a slight grin. Dimples were my kryptonite. I knew I needed to get out of there. He climbed to his feet and shoved his hands in his pockets.

He was tall. Much taller than I expected, dwarfing me as I stood beside him.

"I can give you a ride home. I'm leaving anyway," he offered.

I wasn't drunk enough to forget entirely that horror movies started that way, so I shook my head no. "Stranger danger and all that."

He nodded. "At least let me walk with you."

With the party still raging and the sound mostly muffled, I thought it over. Somehow his presence felt protective, and anyone from the party could drive by me traveling alone. Based on their reaction at the party, it wouldn't be the worst idea to let him tag along. Finally, I nodded. "Yeah, okay. Thank you."

He shrugged. "No need. I want to make sure you get home okay."

We began walking side by side in silence. Once we made it to my street, I decided it was close enough and stopped, turning to face the mystery guy. "My house is just over there." I pointed down the block.

He seemed to take the hint and didn't argue as he stared

down at me, asking, "What's your name?"

What did it matter? "Why?"

He shrugged. "This was the best conversation I've had in a long time. Despite what happened to both of us, I'm glad I met you."

"You won't be back," I reminded him.

He frowned before finally nodding. "I get it."

I took a step back. "Tristan."

"Tristan," he repeated as if tasting the name before pausing. "He didn't kiss you?"

I shook my head, and he stepped forward.

"What are you doing?" I questioned.

"Have you *ever* been kissed?" he murmured.

Again, I shook my head, and he took another step. Licking his lips, he reached out and gripped my chin. I barely had time to register what was happening before he leaned down. When he paused, I didn't pull away. My breath caught as he gently pressed his lips to mine—really a barely-there brush of his lips—before slowly pulling away.

"Now you have." His minty breath coasted over my lips, and my eyes opened just as he stepped back.

When had my eyes closed? "You..."

I wasn't sure what I wanted to say. As far as first kisses went, I sort of liked it, a lot, and wished he'd do it again. This stranger made me feel like all kinds of stoned ass butterflies were swarming in my stomach.

His hand lifted as if he wanted to touch me again, but he paused before lowering it. "It's weird, but I wanted your first kiss to belong to me. I should have asked."

"I could have pulled away," I reminded him. He'd given me time.

His nostrils flared, and his voice roughened. "But you didn't."

"No," I agreed. I already craved more, but he took another step back.

"Tristan, you were an unexpected surprise. I'm almost glad my ex broke things off."

"Almost?" My brow rose.

He grinned again, dimples deepening as he revealed straight white teeth. "Fine. I'm definitely glad. Doesn't that make me shitty or something?"

No. It didn't. "It means you know your worth. He doesn't deserve you."

He ducked his head. "I better get going before he reports my truck sitting outside his house. He probably thinks I'm sulking."

I snorted. "Instead, you're stealing a kiss from a stranger."

He chuckled, the sound deep and raw. "And I don't regret it for a second."

My grin quirked my lips, and he stilled. "You should do that more often."

My brow furrowed. "What?"

"Smile," he said simply, and I went all stupidly fuzzy inside. "Now go home."

"Bossy," I muttered, and it triggered another rich laugh rumbling from his lips. "This was...easier than I expected, maybe because I don't know you and will probably never see you again. Thank you."

Suddenly his jaw clenched again, but his tone was soft. "I'm not going to let him get away with what he did to you."

I smiled at the thought, but he hadn't been able to pry a name from me. Dramatically, I pressed a hand to my chest. "My hero."

He ignored the teasing gesture. "Doing the right thing doesn't make me a hero."

He'd leave and never look back. He'd probably even forget about me. But at that moment, I didn't think about those things. His words were almost enough to convince me he was serious. "It sort of does."

Before he could respond, I spun on my heels and headed home. I could feel him watching me. Maybe I should have been concerned, but something told me he wanted to make sure I got home safely. I glanced over my shoulder once I reached the door, and he nodded before turning away.

I let myself in the house and quietly locked the door. I didn't want my parents to wake up and discover what a mess I was.

Only when I'd cleaned up and was tucked into bed, I realized I'd never gotten his name. The only thing I'd called him was 'Evil Chicken Nugget.' I guess it would do. My lips still tingled from the feel of his lips.

I decided right there that I wouldn't hide who I was. Those people who had stared at me tonight, making me feel small and disgusting, could kiss my ass. I was sad I'd never see that guy again, but if I ever did, I'd tell him what he'd done for me. I could only hope I'd left a similar mark on him too.

Monday, when I went to school, I was met with rumors and given a wide berth as I walked down the hallway. I expected it. What I hadn't expected was the rumor that Brantley had been expelled. That rumor was later confirmed when I was called to the principal's office, where my mom and dad sat in front of his desk, both appearing upset. The guy had been serious, and someone important enough to get the star athlete kicked out of school so close to graduation.

Who the hell was he?

TWO

MEMPHIS

SIXTEEN MONTHS LATER

"DAMN IT," I whispered under my breath as I scanned the field, picking apart the defense's plan to blitz as they crouched low.

The chilly Saturday breeze was rare for an October day in Texas, carrying the stench of the sweaty athletes that were scattered all over the field. Even with the midday sun cutting through the partially cloudy sky, the brisk wind whipped against my exposed face and arms. Still, I was overheated in my football uniform, and several drops of sweat rolled down my temple beneath my helmet.

Sugar Land Stadium was packed with fans—all the seats completely sold out. In a sea of black and gold, the home crowd seemed to battle with the Bengals' fans, wearing orange and white, over who could make the most noise. The near-deafening roar made it difficult for my o-line to hear the play as they took their places in front of me. I gnawed on my mouthpiece.

The uproar had caused a series of botched plays when the strategy had been a hurry-up offense, giving the Bengals little time to prepare. The defense caused me to pause when I saw they'd adjusted their positions as if they knew exactly the play we had planned.

Fuck. I glanced at my o-line again, making a last-minute decision to change the play. We were down to mere seconds before we'd lose yardage for delay of game.

"Kill. Kill," I ground out, demanding a change from the planned play.

The Saints shifted position after I made the new call, and with one second on the play clock, the ball was snapped. The play was fucked from the beginning when the poorly executed handoff dropped to the ground. Muttering a curse, I scrambled to scoop and secure the ball back into my hands. I didn't have time to analyze the mistake. I'd worry about that later when reviewing the tape. Instead, my gaze skipped over players, searching for my go-to wide receivers, Garret and Donnelly. They were the two who had replaced Nash and Shaw this year.

The pressure was closing in around me as the Bengals bulldozed their way through my teammates. I could feel the sack coming like ghost hands skating over my body. The Bengals had one of the most considerable defenses in both weight and height in the league, and my guys were struggling to hold them back while I waited for a clean window to open. The secondary was practically glued to my receivers, and it quickly became clear I had nowhere to go.

The crowd was still loud as hell, and I could barely hear myself think.

I'd waited too long in the pocket and felt more heat than I cared for as fingertips grazed my side. A linebacker grabbed my black jersey, and I bolted, breaking free of the tight hold. Tucking the football tight to my chest, I found a slight crease—a weak spot that offered me a slim chance to break through their defense. I skirted between the massive bodies, hoping to salvage what I could of the play. At a minimum, I needed to get back to the original line of scrimmage.

When two safeties came charging for me, I slid legs first onto the turf, giving myself up to avoid taking any damage. I jerked my gaze to the sideline, noting the yard markers. Not the best run, but I'd managed to pick up two additional yards. The whistle had blown, and Logan Kelley, my most trusted tight end and good friend, hovered above me with his hand held out.

"Off the ground, Hale. Naptime is later." An amused grin twisted his lips, and his dark brown eyes creased at the sides.

I gripped his palm and let him haul me up to my feet. Only an inch shorter than me, Logan was a big guy I was glad to have on my side. Still, I shot him a mock glare. "Thanks, dick."

With a chuckle, he patted my helmet. We quickly lined back up, and I glanced at the game clock. We were down to just under three minutes in the fourth quarter, and it had been a close, back and forth game so far. It shouldn't have been. Statistically, our team was better, not that the play-back film would support that.

I shoved my mouthpiece back in place and wiped my hands on the towel hanging from my pants. The defense looked poised to blitz again, but I was ready for it this time.

I took my place under center with my running back lined up behind me.

The snap was quick, and I immediately hid the ball, shoving it into Ryan's chest as he bulldozed his short, stout frame through the line, finding a perfect gap, and took off. He was tripped up by a last-minute ankle grab but had picked up the first down we'd desperately needed.

We continued working our way down the field as the clock ticked down to the two-minute warning.

In the red zone, I took a shotgun snap and retreated into the pocket once more. Garret ran right and jerked left, leaving him open in a perfectly executed route. I let the ball fly, and he snagged the dart with both hands.

Eyes trained on him, the unexpected impact of a colossal body slamming into my side took me by surprise. I hit the ground hard, breath whooshing from my lungs. I forced myself to roll onto my side to find out the result of the play. With pain coursing through my body, a smile stretched my lips when I watched Garret spike the ball in the end zone. Two refs signaled the touchdown, and my gaze flicked to the scoreboard as six points were added to our total, leaving us now seven points ahead.

Yellow flags littered the ground, and I knew it would be for the late hit that big son of a bitch laid on me. Without a doubt, I'd be feeling that one later.

Naturally, the guy threw his hands in the air as he stupidly argued about his innocence even as the large screen replayed explicitly what had happened.

I was helped to my feet once again by Logan. "You good?"

"Define *good*." I winced, but the adrenaline pumping in my veins muted the pain. He cursed from behind me as I cradled my ribs and chased after my guys, meeting them in the black end zone with *Saints* written in gold. I gripped Garrett's shoulders and shook him hard, ignoring the jolt of pain it brought. "Way to finally show the fuck up, G."

I slapped the back of his helmet, and we jogged off toward the sideline, where our teammates met us with high fives.

Ripping off my helmet, I sucked in deep breaths and

flopped down on the bench. One of the offensive coaches stood in front of me, holding his tablet. "You good, or should we send you to the medical tent?"

Was he joking? Less than two minutes on the clock with a game this close? There wasn't a chance in hell I was leaving the final score up to my backup QB, even if he was a decent player. "I'm good."

He eyed me skeptically. "Memphis—"

"I said I'm good. Whatcha got?" I tilted my chin to the tablet he held.

"Stubborn..." He trailed off as we watched our kicker drill the ball down the center of the uprights for the extra point.

After the play, my coach sighed and drew my attention back to the tablet. I listened attentively, drowning out the screams, cheers, and shouts of my name coming from the seats behind me.

THE COOL WATER from the locker room shower stung as I lathered soap over my battered skin.

"You went down hard." Logan squinted at me as if searching for visible injuries when I glanced over at him in the crowded stall that smelled of bleach, body odor, and a mix of scented soaps.

Mumbled agreements from the team followed.

"That the excuse you're using to eye fuck me?" I cocked a brow.

Logan glared as an answering boom of laughter from the others echoed off the tiled walls. "Fuck you, Hale."

Even though I was giving him a hard time, he was right. I hadn't even begun to feel the aches that would follow. But

I'd suffered much worse hits so I barely noticed the pain anymore. At least we'd won. "I'm just screwing with you. I'm good, or at least I will be."

He nodded as if satisfied and stepped out from beneath the spray. "What are we doing tonight to celebrate?"

After quickly rinsing off, I followed behind him as we each snagged a towel and tied them around our waists.

"First, I'm gonna pass the fuck out," I replied. My stomach decided to growl loud as hell, causing Logan to smirk at me over his shoulder as he scrubbed his dark auburn hair dry. "Scratch that. I'm going to grab some food, *then* pass out. Not sure about later." I shrugged as I stopped in front of my locker, popped it open, and pulled out my clothes. "Why? What's up?"

"Party at Sigma Chi," Logan said from behind me as others joined us. "The usual. You coming?"

"Probably. I don't have any other plans." I dropped the towel and tugged on my boxer briefs, then jeans. Usually, I'd have my parents waiting at the gates on game days and would be forced to listen to my dad critique the entire game. Thankfully, my super-fan parents had a wealthy family moving into the city, so they were busy today trying to close one of the many homes they had for sale.

"Sweet. I'm outta here," Logan said as he bumped into my shoulder when he passed me. I held back a wince from the ache settling into my muscles. "Shit, sorry."

I waved off the apology. "See you later."

"Later, man." With a chagrined expression, he left the locker room.

Once dressed, I said goodbye to the guys in the locker room and made my way to the parking lot where my truck was parked. Dents and scratches littered the body, and dirt coated the once shiny blue paint. Just the way I liked her.

Gingerly, I tossed my bag into the passenger seat and climbed into the super cab. As I cranked the engine, my stomach sent another reminder that I was fucking starving.

I headed toward the sandwich shop across the street from campus. I'd regularly met my friends there last year, but even after they'd all graduated, I'd stuck to the routine. After a short drive, I pulled up to the small restaurant.

As I stepped down from my truck, my phone buzzed in my pocket. After shutting and locking my baby, I fished my cell out and wasn't surprised at all to see Nash's name flashing on the screen.

I answered and pressed it to my ear as I approached the glass front door. "What's up?"

"Not you apparently," the cocky asshole, and my closest friend, replied. "Why'd you take a hit like that?"

My brow cocked as I opened the door, immediately assaulted by the scent of baking bread and spices that only fueled my hunger as I stepped inside. "I didn't exactly ask for it."

"Do I need to come back and talk to your receivers? If they'd run clean routes, that wouldn't have happened." Nash regularly critiqued the team's performance, specifically the wide receivers.

"Your ego has only gotten worse since going pro. Not everyone has natural talent," I replied as I stepped close to the counter, scanning the menu posted above the register.

"And there you go stroking my ego." The smug tone of his voice wasn't surprising. "You only have yourself to blame."

"We are still trying to hit our stride. They did fine." The cashier, who was also the owner, smiled as she headed toward where I waited. "Hang on, Nash."

"The usual?" she asked.

"Yes, please. But can you double the meat?"

With a knowing grin, she nodded. "You got it. You want a table or to-go?"

"To-go, please." Once she walked off, I stepped back and lifted the phone.

"But for real," Nash was still ranting, and I wondered if he'd even heard me put him on hold. "That shouldn't have happened."

I sighed. "It was a late hit. Not our guys' fault."

He continued to critique the new starting players that had filled his, Shaw's, and Bishop's vacated spots. As he talked, I tuned out and scanned the restaurant, startling when I collided with ice blue eyes thinly lined with black eyeliner or something. His frosty eyes narrowed, and I forced a bored expression in a way that had become second nature over the last year and a half as I continued to look around the room. But in that half-second, I'd cataloged everything about him, as usual.

Tristan Stafford sat in a booth by himself, sipping on what appeared to be a strawberry milkshake while he held his phone in his other hand. His raven-colored hair hung long on one side of his face, while the hair on the other side was shaved close to his scalp. Short, slim, pale, and emo vibes in spades—he wasn't my type. Except, apparently, he was. When I'd kissed him the night I'd found him collapsed beneath that tree, I had wanted him to have the experience, but selfishly I'd wanted it for myself too. I was drawn to him in a way I had never been attracted to another person. He knew more about me than anyone else ever had. But he didn't know that.

Did I try to avoid Tristan? Yes. Did I notice him anyway? Also, yes. His appearance was different in many ways from that night I'd kissed him, but also the same, which made staying away from him harder than I'd thought it would be. Maybe it was because he'd told me he felt comfortable unloading his baggage on a stranger. Or possibly because it would force me to examine my own issues after I'd decided not to out myself as bisexual to the world. Either way, I'd made the decision to maintain my distance. As a junior at Sugar Land and Tristan a year behind me, that meant there was still a long time I'd have to maintain the charade.

I didn't think Tristan recognized me from that night. But if he did, he probably thought I was an asshole, which was arguably accurate.

"Hey, you there, Hale?" Nash's voice dragged my attention away when I'd completely forgotten he was on the phone.

"Yeah, sorry." I cleared my throat. "You ready for tomorrow's game?" I asked, trying to stay involved in the conversation. My gaze flicked back to Tristan, risking getting caught, but he was focused on his phone, tapping on the screen. It was seriously fucked up how badly I wanted to know who he was talking to. Was it a guy? A hookup—something my nosy ass was aware he often did. Did Tristan have a boyfriend?

And most importantly, why did I care so much? He was just a guy, no matter what had happened between us. I swallowed hard and forced my gaze away, trying to shake off the memory of our brief time together.

Nash scoffed. "Have I ever not been ready for something?"

"Rendon comes to mind," I pointed out. The former playboy hadn't seen Shaw's younger brother coming, and he'd almost royally fucked that up before their relationship even began. Speaking of Shaw, I wasn't sure why'd I'd had a short-lived thing for him when I'd first transferred to Sugar Land. I snuck another quick peek at Tristan, knowing that was a lie. Shaw had been the complete opposite of Tristan, and I'd been looking for a distraction from my inability to stop thinking about Tristan all of the time. It hadn't worked.

Nash scoffed, grabbing my attention again. "I really hate you sometimes."

I snorted. "Nah, you don't."

"Whatever. Back to the game, your receivers..."

Sighing, I let him rant as I waited for my food.

THREE
TRISTAN

"JERK FACE SMOKING HOT SKEET NINJA," I muttered under my breath when Memphis's navy-blue gaze swept over the sandwich shop, not even with much more than a slight pause when his eyes met mine as I watched him. His holy jockness seemed to look right through me as if I was a fucking ghost. Like always. And no, I didn't think he was actually a god, unlike the rest of the population. However, I wouldn't mind dropping to my knees to worship his dick. I scowled as I jerked my stare from him and back to the phone in my hand where I had a message waiting from my best friend, Rendon.

Not even sure why I was surprised by Memphis's lack of acknowledgment after almost a year and a half had passed since I'd set eyes on the asshole on campus for the first time. While we'd never technically met, not with formal introductions anyway, I had been around Nash and Rendon enough that there was no way Memphis was completely oblivious to my existence. We'd been in the same room with the same group of friends countless times, yet I might as well have been invisible.

I might have had a thing for him last year, but I wasn't into him anymore. My cock, however, seemed to be on a separate page. A different planet, really. The sight of him with denim hugging his ass in just the right places caused it to thicken in my tight jeans. With dark chestnut brown hair that he often wore beneath a backward hat, pale skin that only held the slightest bronzed tan, and tall with lean, defined muscles, and dimples—*fuck me*, the dimples—Memphis *was* nice to look at. But definitely not worth my time. Annoyed, I brushed my hair out of my eyes with a huff.

My phone chirped again, this time not a text. I swiped the notification, and a beat of excitement jolted through me as the *dating* app popped up. The app I used notified me when someone who also used it was nearby. Even though a distraction was welcome after Memphis's dismissal, it would have to wait. I clicked back to Rendon's message in response to mine before Memphis had walked into the restaurant.

BF Foreva: *I got written up again for being late. Otherwise, everything's good.*

I'd asked how his job at the coffee house in Denver was going. It was still weird not having him around since he'd moved to Colorado, where Nash had been drafted months ago into the pro league.

Me: *Awesome. Any hot regulars?*

BF Foreva: **eye roll emoji**

Me: *That's not an answer.*

BF Foreva: *Um, have you seen my boyfriend? Why would I notice other guys?*

Rendon had a point. Nash was hot. Not as hot as Memphis, though. I scolded myself for the betraying thought. It wasn't enough to keep me from peeking up at

Memphis, who was talking on his phone while standing near the counter waiting for his food, I guessed.

I wondered if he was talking to some girl. Though I'd never actually spotted him with anyone, and there were oddly zero rumors floating around campus, I wasn't naive enough to believe he was a saint. Well, I mean, he was a Saint, but not a *saint*. Whatever.

Mentally slapping myself because he was stealing my attention again, I returned my focus to my phone as I sucked on the straw stuffed into a thick strawberry milkshake. I reread Rendon's message before replying.

Me: *Fine. When are you coming back to visit?*

BF Foreva: *Not sure, but with Nash being so busy, we probably won't make it back until Thanksgiving. Maybe we can meet up then.*

Me: *You better, or I'm gonna start thinking you don't miss me.*

BF Foreva: *I'll let you know when I know. My break's over, so I gotta get back to work. Some of us have jobs.*

I glared at the dig aimed at my unemployment. Not going to lie—with my parents happy to pay my tuition, getting a job was low on my list of priorities. Instead, I was taking extra classes.

Me: *Whatever. Talk to you later.*

BF Foreva: *Later.*

Clicking out of my texts, I pulled up the notification from the dating-slash-hookup app. I frowned when I clicked on the profile—the nearly bare profile.

Up4it

6'5

Lean but muscled.

Hookup only. Hit me up.

It was enough to pique my interest. Of course, that

was probably due to the profile picture of a nicely sculpted, pale chest with flat light brown nipples, muscular arms, and shoulders dusted with a light peppering of freckles. There was even a small birthmark low on his toned stomach that oddly resembled the state of Washington. Too bad there wasn't a picture of his face. My profile also portrayed a headless body shot—safety and all.

A thread of curiosity and suspicion snagged my thoughts, and I shot a glimpse at Memphis, quickly studying him. He fit the profile since his build was similar, but he was straight, so I knew it wasn't him. It was, however, enough for me to pursue a conversation with whoever was nearby.

Just as I went to message the guy, loud voices filled the shop as a large group of guys stepped inside. Some were tall, but not six-five. It wasn't unusual for guys to embellish their looks online, so my gaze swept over the newcomers, now knowing one of them had to be responsible for the alert.

To test the theory, I returned to the profile again and hit the message icon.

T-Man 10023: *More pics?*

Quickly, my gaze shot to the boisterous group of guys again. None of them even pulled out their phones. *Damn.*

When a response didn't come before I finished my milkshake, I sighed and scooted out of the booth. Stuffing my phone in my pocket, I crossed the restaurant, pausing to toss the plastic cup in the trash before heading for the door.

It appeared that Memphis, no longer on the phone, was leaving at the same time. With a paper bag in hand, he made it to the door first. My gaze dipped to his ass, but only for a second. He opened the door, and the big jerk, to my surprise, held it open for me.

Maybe there was hope for him yet. I grinned up at him. "Thanks."

Emotionless, he briefly glanced down at me and gave a curt nod before heading for his truck parked near the curb. I glared at his back and turned right toward the side parking lot, passing by the coffee shop Rendon had worked at last year. I would honestly wonder if Memphis was even capable of speaking if I hadn't heard that husky voice talking to other people. But to me? Not a single peep.

I stalked off to my car, clutching my thick puffer coat tighter around me. The sun was out, but the temperature held in the low fifties, and the cold was not my friend. It was early October in Texas, which meant the state was having a hormonal mood swing.

I hit the key fob as I neared my sporty red car that sat low to the ground. After tossing my phone in the cup holder, I settled into the tight black leather bucket seat and shut the door harder than necessary. I was in cahoots with Texas because I was in a mood, too, thanks to Memphis. He shouldn't have held the door open and let me think for half a second that he even registered my presence.

As soon as I started the engine, the familiar chime of a notification came through. Interested once again, I snatched my phone and clicked on the icon, wondering if the guy had finally responded. He had.

Up4it: *You first.*

I shrugged. This guy wasn't the first possibly skittish one I'd contacted. And if he was nearby, maybe he'd clear my head and help me forget about stupid-hot Memphis.

Luckily, I already had a dick pic handy for moments like this. Without hesitation, I uploaded my best shot and hit send. The response was immediate.

Up4it: *Not exactly what I meant.*

My eyebrows scrunched together, and I frowned. My profile picture was a sweet shot of my ass in a pair of black boxer briefs. Maybe he was a face guy. But now that he had a picture of my cock—a fucking worship-worthy pic—he'd have to ante up first.

T-Man 10023: *You gotta send me something first. Your dick would be nice.*

Another instant reply.

Up4it: *I want to see your face.*

I sighed as I became almost certain the guy was wasting my time.

T-Man 10023: *Well, I hope you're stellar in the sack because your pre-hookup skills are terrible. You've heard of negotiation, right?*

I quickly attached a picture that included my face I'd taken a few weeks ago just before I'd headed out to a nearby club.

T-Man 10023: *There. Now, you sending back a pic or what?*

My car idled in the parking lot for a few minutes before I gave up and set my phone aside again. His loss.

Driving away from the sandwich shop, I headed for my apartment. I had a party to get ready for. Maybe there I'd have better luck finding someone who was interested.

I probably needed a hobby or something to keep myself busy. One that didn't include constantly looking for sex. But for the last year and a half, I'd been trying to prove to myself I didn't care what other people thought. I had a sex life, so what? I was careful, and I didn't owe anyone an explanation. My thoughts weren't new. Sometimes I wondered why I turned to hookups when I was feeling slighted or even just bored. But when I seriously considered it, I was fully aware it had everything to do with what had happened in high school. Still, I wasn't doing anything wrong.

If it ain't broke, don't fix it. I decided the old adage made perfect sense as I drove down the busy highway.

My apartment was just outside of town, close enough to campus that commuting was easy and just far enough to get away when I wanted. I turned into the parking lot and pulled into my reserved space beneath a metal awning. Scooting from the seat, I headed for the nearby stairs. My unit was on the second floor, and I took the steps at an unhurried pace.

When I opened the door, the scent from the fresh cream-colored paint that lingered in the air greeted me, but not as strong as when I'd first moved in. The space was small with one bedroom and one bath, mainly due to the tiny kitchen nook and living room being divided by a thick wall. What it lacked in size, it made up for with updated stainless-steel appliances and the softest plush beige carpet.

Dropping my keys on the granite kitchen counter, I passed by my gray cloth couch and headed straight for the shower. After I stripped down, I didn't waste time stepping beneath the hot spray.

Left high and dry by the mystery guy through the app combined with mental images of everything Memphis, I propped myself against the tiled wall and wrapped my other hand around my hard cock. As I jacked off, it was no surprise that despite trying otherwise, I remembered the soft lips that had brushed against mine for the first time—a face I couldn't picture. Seconds into the fantasy of those lips wrapped around my cock, the image morphed into Memphis on his knees, deep blue eyes lifted as he watched me fall apart. He sucked me down his throat, and I came hard, panting afterward as I caught my breath. It was always the same fantasy, no matter how much I tried to think of other things.

"Every fucking time," I muttered as I swiped the soap from the shelf.

Still frustrated and now angry at myself, I scrubbed my body clean with the cinnamon-scented body wash, rinsed it all away, and dried off. With a plush black towel secured around my waist, I entered my room. Posters of my favorite bands hung on the walls, and rows of horror films lined the shelves next to my large flat-screen TV. I dropped onto the mattress of my ridiculously comfortable queen-sized bed and snagged my laptop from the side table. I needed to tackle my homework and waste some time before I'd have to get ready for the party.

Flipping onto my stomach, I pulled up the half-written document. I began working on my essay on the human body. The mind, specifically. History of Psychology was the one class I actually looked forward to each week. Our brains were complex, especially when someone had suffered a traumatic event. And hadn't we all in one way or another? That was the reason it challenged me when very few subjects did.

After finishing the draft, I pushed the laptop aside and scrolled through social media. Bored, I debated messaging Rendon again, but he had a life now. I couldn't expect him just to drop whatever he was doing to talk to me every time I had nothing to keep me busy, which was often.

With a dramatic sigh, I pushed from the bed and dug through my closet, trying to decide what to wear to this stupid frat party. I'd promised my friend—or, more accurately, occasional wingman—that I'd go. Since Rendon had left, I didn't really have anyone to hang out with. I pulled out a black shirt and dark jeans as I considered Martin and why I occasionally hung out with him when ninety percent of the time, one or both of us disappeared without the other.

That's probably what I needed. A real friend. Someone to make life a little less mundane. But I had to face it—I wasn't everyone's cup of tea. The flavor could be too strong and definitely an acquired taste.

I tossed my clothes on the bed and dropped the towel. As I slipped on my black briefs, my phone rang. I sighed when I saw my parents' number on the screen. They hadn't checked in on me in over twenty-four hours, which was a record for the overprotective duo. Ever since the video incident, they'd taken it upon themselves to monitor my every move, or at least they would if they could. In the grand scheme of things, I knew I'd face more significant obstacles than what had happened senior year. As traumatized as I'd been the day the video had circled through the entire student body—before the stranger had sat next to me, comforting me—my parents had taken it much harder.

Answering, I turned on the speakerphone. "Hey, Mom."

"Hi, baby." My mom breathed out as if relieved I'd answered. "I just wanted to check on you today."

As always. "I'm fine, Mom. You guys really don't need to worry so much."

Her voice was strained. "We can't help it. After everything—"

"I know," I interrupted as I slid my shirt over my head. "But I promise I'm careful." It was almost the truth, but I refused to live my life metaphorically bundled in bubble wrap to protect me from the world, which I'm sure they'd both prefer.

With a troubled sigh, she relented. "Call us if you need anything."

"You know I will. And Dad, I know you're listening too. I swear I'm fine."

His stern reply followed. "We just want you to be safe."

Pushing my hair away from my face, I breathed a frustrated groan. "I get it, but I'll let y'all know if I need help. I promise."

Seemingly satisfied, my parents ended the call after a few more reassurances, and I finished getting ready for the party.

I finished dressing, fixed my hair, and traced around my pale blue eyes with eyeliner after checking out my ass in the full-length mirror glued on the bathroom door. By the time Martin texted me to meet up with him at the frat house, I still hadn't gotten a message back from Up4it. I sighed, officially accepting the hookup was a lost cause. Back to the plan of trying to find someone at the party to spend a few hours with in bed.

A friend is what I really needed, I reminded myself as I stared into my mirrored reflection.

"Behave yourself," I hissed, knowing damn well I never listened to my own advice.

FOUR
TRISTAN

"WHY DO I even bother with college parties," I mumbled to myself from the shadowy corner I'd been leaning against for the past hour. The stench of sweat in the air mingled with perfume and cologne, a mix that made it hard to breathe. The music pounded through the sound system in the darkened Sigma Chi house where bodies ground together, only to be seen under the black fluorescent lights. Around the corner, I knew the kitchen held an impressive collection of liquor bottles that sat half-empty. The drunk students yelling over the thumping bass echoed the ringing in my ears.

Completely sober, I scoured the room for potential, scanning guy to guy—the ones that weren't currently lip-locked with girls or grinding against their asses. Jocks and the preppy type were the usual fare at these parties. Tonight was no different, and I found my interest waning as usual.

I rarely drank, but when I did, I toed the line at being buzzed. Getting drunk had lost its appeal when I realized I made dumb decisions when intoxicated. And I'd need to be lit to consider the guys filling the spacious room.

It was easier than one might think to find a guy willing to fool around on campus, even if they were only curious. But I preferred the quick and fast method that came with the app. It wasn't like I needed or wanted to get to know a guy. I didn't have time or the mental energy for that. Plus, my trust issues were likely to be impressive to any psychologist. Only once had I ever trusted someone enough to tell them the truth, and only because I knew I'd never see him again. I shoved the memory of that night away. Thinking of him always fucked with my head. In that brief time I'd had with him, he'd set an impossible bar for any regular guy to meet. Not that I was searching for anything serious. Speaking of seriousness, the throbbing in my temples had started to increase, and I was over the party.

Even though I'd shown up with Martin, he'd ditched me not even fifteen minutes later to hook up with some guy he was boning regularly. Not that I cared. I rarely hung out with him. I reminded myself for the tenth time that's precisely why I needed a new friend now that Rendon was gone.

I was bored, and options were lacking anyway. Mind made up to bail, I kicked away from the wall and headed for the front door. As soon as the door closed behind me, the sounds from inside muted to a dull hum, and I sighed in relief. Grateful for the clean air, I took several deep breaths.

That reprieve lasted a total of thirty seconds before I spotted Memphis leaning against a concrete pillar on the front porch, wearing another pair of jeans paired with a worn black shirt similar to my own. He spoke words I couldn't hear, gesturing wildly, with one of his football buddies, Logan, whom I recognized thanks to my best friend dragging me to a few Saints' games last year. Memphis ran his fingers thoughtlessly through his thick hair as he laughed.

The husky sound sent a sharp spike of lust straight to my cock, and I glared at him, even though he wasn't even looking at me. The plan to bypass the asshole without giving him another chance to piss me off came to a grinding halt when he glanced at me. He barely paused after he spotted me before he turned back to his buddy. A quiet growl crawled up my throat.

Already sexually frustrated and irritated from our run-in at the sandwich shop, I stalked over to the brute, my feet moving without my permission. Coming to an abrupt stop mere feet in front of him, I huffed out a breath, trying desperately to ignore the scent of warm spices that almost made me forget how pissed I was.

Memphis jerked around, and his eyebrows shot up as he stared down at me, something like shock painting his features. I waited, then waited a few seconds more, but was met with silence. His teammate cleared his throat, but I didn't spare him a single glance, laser-focused on Memphis, as he tightened his lips as if he refused to speak.

"You could say hello, you know," I snapped. "You don't have to be such an egotistical asshole, thinking you're too good to acknowledge the incredibly sexy gay boy—which I am, by the way, in case you were too busy to notice."

Memphis studied me, quiet at first, and then appeared to reluctantly deem me worthy of a one-word reply. "Hello."

I froze for half a second. Memphis had actually responded. His voice sounded familiar and infuriatingly drenched in sex appeal. Too bad Memphis was a dick because the guy it reminded me of had been amazing.

I rolled my eyes and thickened my voice with enough

sarcasm to make every teenager in America green with envy. "Hello to you too. I'm Tristan, by the way, in case your overinflated ego was curious. You know, the guy you ignore every time we are in the same space." I paused and mumbled under my breath, "Ass monkey yak, likely with an envious case of elephant dick."

What a waste. And why was I comparing him to animals? I frowned.

"On that note, I think I'll go find my boyfriend." Logan chuckled, but neither of us spared him a glance as he walked back inside, leaving us alone on the front porch.

Memphis tilted his head as he seemed to peruse my face. "Have I done something to piss you off?"

"Everything," I snapped, and his lips turned down at the sides. Had he seriously not ever truly noticed me? I shook my head, refusing to believe that as many times as we'd crossed paths last year. "Never mind."

Memphis stared at me silently again, and I narrowed my eyes once more. He didn't need to know that despite being a rude dick, he was also hardcore spank bank material. Starting from his tennis shoes, I quickly scanned his ridiculously perfect body. I didn't even bother with subtlety. It wasn't my strong suit anyway. Once I reached his eyes again, Memphis's lips twitched in amusement. My annoyance spiked, but he surprised me when he spoke. "That's a lot of judgment coming from someone that doesn't even know me."

When he crossed his arms over his chest, I mirrored the movement and blew my hair that had stubbornly fallen across my face. "I know your type."

"My type?" He narrowed his eyes. "What *type* would that be?"

I shrugged. "The type that thinks they are god's gift to women and can't be bothered to acknowledge people beneath him. It's not like you haven't seen me before. Or maybe I *am* that invisible to you, which makes you crazy for obvious reasons." I dropped one arm, gesturing toward my body with a sweeping wave. "Am I wrong?"

Memphis bit his full lower lip and gave a thoughtful nod while humming. "Ego? Truth. It depends on what we're talking about. In bed? Definitely. On the field?" He cocked a brow. "No brainer. But I'm not sure what else you have me labeled as, so unless you want to fill me in..."

I scowled at the blatant dismissal of what I'd said about his lack of acknowledging me. Instead of pointing out the omission, I focused on what he *had* addressed. Of course, Memphis thought he was mind-blowing in the sack, which he likely was. But he'd never had me. I'd already given him too much of my time.

"No thanks," I finally responded. Spinning on my heels, I intended to leave in the same manner Memphis always had, as if he wasn't worth my time. I had barely taken a step off the porch before I whipped back around, finding him staring right at me. Sometimes I really hated my lack of self-control. I'd think about that later. "But also, since you're under some misguided idea you're king of between-the-sheet-fun-stuff, I'll have you know that you couldn't impress me. I'm crazy talented. And flexible."

A muffled groan vibrated through the air, an indecipherable sound I figured meant he didn't believe me. He should, because it was true.

"I'm Memphis, in case your too-quick-to-judge ass was curious," he said lazily, almost echoing my words, and lifted a brow. "Guess we both have our flaws."

I'd taken another step away, but his words stopped me in my tracks. Anger bubbled in my chest, and I glared. "Listen to me, you lord of the jizz stompers, you *do* ignore me. Every time you happen to pass by me, which seems to be an awful lot. Not that I've particularly noticed, by the way. Just because I'm gay doesn't automatically turn you into catnip and me into a junkie kitten. You just happen to be a giant muscled asshole who's hard to miss. But I repeat, I have *not* noticed."

Memphis's eyebrows continued to arch high on his forehead. "Yes, I can *clearly* see how you haven't noticed. But I wasn't aware I'd made such an impression on you."

I bristled and narrowed my eyes. "You haven't."

"No? Seems like some pretty strong opinions from someone who doesn't notice the giant muscled asshole and whatever else you called me." His brow dipped. "I don't even know what the other things mean."

Well then, he wasn't astute. I scoffed. "Whatever. I have things and people to do."

Memphis scowled, and his voice went as rigid as his body stiffened. "Who?" He seemed to gather his composure as he relaxed. "I meant *what*. What do you have to do that's more important than this stimulating conversation we are having?"

I wasn't exactly sure what I'd just witnessed, probably a temper tantrum at being dismissed. "Things. *People*. Like I said." Why did it matter to him anyway? "Whatever I feel like, that doesn't include talking to your not-sexy-at-all, self-important royal dickness."

Memphis rubbed his chest as if wounded, but then a crooked grin stretched across his face, causing that dimple to appear. "Ouch. That might have hurt if it wasn't clear that you actually do think I'm sexy."

Another scowl slammed into place on my face, and I started to worry if being around Memphis would cause premature wrinkling. Maybe I should have just kept walking, but my mouth had a mind of its own. "I do *not* think you're sexy. At all." Memphis's grin grew along with my irritation. "Whatever. Party's lame. I'm out."

"You're seriously leaving?" The smile fell, replaced by a frown.

"That is generally what '*I'm out*' means." I tilted my head. "I'm already *out* the other way."

Memphis's mouth opened and closed right before a breath rushed from his lungs. "Do you want to go do something?"

My brain must have its wires completely fried because it sounded like Memphis just asked me to voluntarily do something with him. "Um... What?"

"My ego is too big to be content with someone hating me. It seems I need to change someone's opinion of me." He leaned back against the pillar, shoving his hands in his pockets.

"And why would I want to do that?" Folding my arms over my chest again, I tried to figure out what his game was. Why the sudden interest? And he seemed to be pretty comfortable messing with me about this *imagined* attraction I felt toward him.

Memphis yawned as if the topic was boring him. "You have plans tomorrow?"

My first instinct was to say I did. But curiosity was burning a hole in my brain. "Depends on the next words out of your mouth."

"Ever been mudding?" he asked, surprising me.

Growing up in Texas, I knew what mudding was, but seriously? "Why the fuck would I ever want to do that?"

"You have an issue with getting a little dirty?" Memphis raised a challenging brow that made my spine stiffen.

Oh, he wanted to play word games. I could do that. I dropped my voice to a low purr. "I like getting plenty dirty. Just not the kind you mean."

Memphis groaned again before shaking his head. "I'll pick you up in the morning."

Do what now? "When did I agree to your proposal exactly?"

Memphis scanned me head to toe, eliciting a shiver that raced over my skin. He deepened his voice lower than mine as if everything was a fucking competition. I should have expected as much from a football player. "You backing down? Ready to admit I'm dirtier than you?"

Not a chance in hell. He was goading me. I knew it and still took the bait. Why? Because Memphis was hot. And wasn't I supposed to be trying to find a friend? My gaze narrowed on his. Yes, yes I was, but not with him. Still... "I don't want one single speck of mud on me."

I immediately regretted the words. Why had I just said that?

Memphis made a poor attempt to stifle a grin. "I promise. Not a *speck* of mud will touch you."

Slowly I nodded, trying to figure out why I agreed to this. I said as much out loud. "I have zero idea why I agreed to this."

Memphis shrugged. "No takebacks."

I paused as the stupid situation I was putting myself into settled in my thoughts. But I was stubborn, and I'd never back down from the challenge in his tone. "I'm not changing my mind."

"Give me your number," he said as he pulled his phone from his pocket, and my mouth opened to tell him I didn't take orders from him. Memphis sighed, reading me before I made a sound. "Or you can just put mine in yours."

I roughly jerked my phone from my pocket too, and Memphis rattled off his number. As I continued tapping on my screen to create a new contact, I glanced up. A cocky smirk twisted his lips. Somehow he appeared to still think he'd won this battle. Honestly, I wasn't sure what the hell had just happened between us. I shot him my smug grin. "I'm not sure why you're smiling, but then I guess you can't see what I saved your number as."

His smile dropped. "What did you put?"

I locked my phone and stuffed it back in my pocket. "Nope. Not telling."

"I'll find out eventually," he vowed. "Might as well tell me now."

"You can't get everything you want."

"Truth," he muttered just loud enough for me to hear.

I chewed on the inside of my cheek, wanting to ask him what he meant, but forcing myself not to voice the question. He'd likely try to barter for the super-secret name on my phone. It was not happening. *Captain Jock-o-potamus* was under lock and key. Or phone and password. Whatever.

I took a step backward toward the street where my car was parked.

Noticing my slow retreat, he winked. "I'll see you in the morning."

"It's the weekend. I better not see you until after noon." I turned and started across the lawn before he could argue.

"Dress warm," he called out, but I pretended not to hear him.

The drive back to my apartment seemed shorter than usual as I replayed the entire interaction with Memphis. It made no sense. How did I go from being ignored to making plans with him for tomorrow? It wasn't like I planned on following through with them anyway. Memphis didn't know where I lived, and he didn't even have my phone number. I just wouldn't call him.

Problem solved.

FIVE

MEMPHIS

SO MUCH FOR my plan to avoid Tristan, I thought as I tucked my hands into the pouch of my Saints hoodie. Gravel crunched under my feet as I headed toward my mud-crusted truck parked in my unpaved driveway. Out of all the properties my family owned, this one was the one they loathed the most. Since I refused to use their money as much as possible, it was also the only one I could afford. Its location outside of town and being set back from the country road, well into the tree line, was just a bonus.

Climbing into the driver's seat, I immediately started the engine and set the heat on high. I shivered as I fought the cold seeping into my bones. As I waited for the cab to heat, my mind drifted back to the sandwich shop and the unexpected message Tristan had sent through that hookup app. The whole exchange could have been prevented if it had been turned off like usual. If I wasn't careful, forgetting to shut it off would out me at some point.

I was worried that Tristan had figured out he was messaging me but, evidently, he hadn't. He was blunt enough that he would have called my ass out if he'd realized it was actually me.

When I'd asked the guy for a picture, I really had meant one of his face. Based on his profile description and Tristan being so close, I was almost sure it was him and only wanted to confirm it. Honestly, I should have expected Tristan to be forward and send me a dick pic. But it wasn't just any pic. It was a fucking *pierced* dick pic. That memory alone was the only defense I had for making the rash decision to invite him to hang out.

The second the photo lit up the screen, I hadn't been prepared at all for the way my cock had hardened or the way my balls demanded I take him up on his offer to fuck. Yes, I was aware that I was attracted to him. But the need that had tightened my sac was a shock. So instead, I bailed on the conversation. I couldn't simply hook up with Tristan. Not with our past and the looming secret between us—one he didn't even know existed. It wasn't right. Not to mention I wasn't a fan of sticking my dick in anyone I ran into regularly, and unfortunately, our paths always seemed to cross.

All those plans and promises to myself to avoid Tristan had gone straight out the window when he'd called me out at the party. I'd found myself wanting to show him who I was because I hated the way he saw me. I guess I could understand why he might see me that way, based on how I'd ignored him. But he didn't know the whole truth.

Now I couldn't keep that promise I'd made to myself. Staying away was not an option since I'd made Tristan feel invisible. Like he didn't matter at all. The only thing I could do was try to fix it and stop myself from looking at the picture again. I had already failed that one multiple times, even before I'd gone to bed right after shooting my load all over my stomach. I hadn't ever come that hard in less than a minute.

Groaning, I scrubbed my hand over my face, scraping over the short stubble I hadn't bothered to shave. I couldn't continue to put off the inevitable, so I messed with the radio, turned up the volume, and drove toward the road with heavy bass thumping through the speakers.

With my mind preoccupied with how today would go, the fifteen-minute drive to Tristan's apartment complex passed in a blur. Would I be able to change his mind? Could I convince him I wasn't just the conceited football player he thought I was?

Before I was ready, I pulled into a space close to his unit and slid out of my truck. Tugging my black Saints beanie lower over my ears, I took the sidewalk to the stairs that led to the second floor.

Once I stood in front of his door, I hesitated to knock. *What the fuck am I doing?*

"No idea," I muttered under my breath just as I tapped my knuckles against the door.

No answer. No sounds of footsteps on the other side either. I knocked harder. Without warning, the door swung open, and a pair of bright blue eyes, hooded with sleep, sprang open with shock. Other than the night we'd met, I'd never seen Tristan's eyes devoid of eyeliner. And that night, his eyes had been red and puffy. He appeared younger with innocent wide eyes. I ground my teeth and swallowed hard as a mental image of that fresh face staring up at me with his lips wrapped— *Shit, he's talking to me.*

Those clear eyes narrowed. "What in the actual dick suck box are you doing here?"

The actual, what? I didn't bother to ask, positive his

answer wouldn't make sense anyway. "I told you I'd be here this morning to pick you up."

"And I told you not before noon." He glanced around me, taking in the early pale light of day before his gaze whipped back to mine. "And how did you know where I live?"

Frowning at his question, I replied, "You gave me the address."

Not only had he given it to me, but Tristan had texted me first. *You better not come get me. I'm serious, Memphis Hale, lord of the football groupies...* And followed it with *Here's my address.*

It was absolutely the weirdest text that had ever shown up on my phone. Even though the number displayed wasn't attached to a name, I'd known it was his weird ass anyway.

Tristan scowled. "No, I didn't."

"Yeah, before I left, I texted you, and you told me."

He squinted before stepping back. "Stay right there."

Of course, the minute he turned around and disappeared down the hall, I stepped inside and shut the door. Tristan's place was tidier than I expected. The all-gray theme didn't come as a surprise. Nor did the black and white wall art. A stack of magazines rested on the coffee table. Curious, I strolled over and began leafing through the pile of old Rolling Stone issues.

"Oh my god," Tristan whisper-shouted from behind me. "Boundaries. They are a thing, you know?"

I turned around and smirked at the scowl he shot me before I glanced at his hand, where his fingers were curled tightly around his phone.

"So? Do you believe me now?" I asked.

"Kind of hard to dispute it when I'm looking at the texts. But I was like asleep, so they don't count. Therefore, you should not know where I live. And you definitely should not be here before noon."

I bit back a smile. "Too bad. Asleep or not, you gave me the address and even said okay when I told you I was leaving the house a while ago."

Tristan stomped over and tore the magazine from my hand. "Get your giant paws off my things. They are currently jock-free. Like the highest power intended."

When Tristan tossed it back on top of the stack, I did my best to stifle a laugh, but apparently, I did a shit job because Tristan glared.

"Go get ready. I won't contaminate your stuff." I had the unfortunate urge to kiss that scowl straight off his pouty lips. Before I could give in and likely be slapped or something, I took him by his shoulders, spun him around, and gave him a slight nudge toward the hall.

I expected an argument, but rather than tell me off again, he stomped back down the hall, hollering over his shoulder, "Touch my things and die!"

"I won't," I lied. When I heard the click of his bedroom door closing, I walked around the living room, studying the white-framed photos of his family on the mantel above the faux fireplace. I recognized their faces. Before I'd called his high school's administration the following Monday after meeting him, I'd browsed his social media. He hadn't been hard to find. One of the pictures caught my eye, and I simply stared. It wasn't taken that long ago, maybe just a few years. He looked almost exactly as I remembered him from that night, minus the puffy red eyes that had tugged at my heart in a way I'd never experienced before. Tristan's hair was shorter, and his demeanor relaxed as he stood between his parents in front of a brown brick home.

I ran my finger lightly over his face. It was striking how

much he'd changed from the time the picture had been taken. I hated Brantley O'Brien, and I'd been happy as shit to throw my status in the college football world around to get him kicked out of school. I didn't feel bad about it. Honestly, he had deserved it.

The scent of cinnamon arrived just as a throat cleared behind me. "It is quickly becoming clear you are incapable of following simple instructions. I demand breakfast as penance."

I spun around, grinning when I found him dressed in black jeans and a long sleeve t-shirt. That shit was going to be destroyed by late morning. "Hungry?" I smirked.

"Starving." He unhooked his coat from the wall. "Coffee too."

"You ready?" I asked as I headed for the door.

Tristan scoffed as he buttoned his jacket. "*Resigned* is the word you're looking for."

I chuckled as we left his apartment.

"THIS IS WHERE I DIE, isn't it?" Tristan was damn near hyperventilating, sitting in the passenger seat as I spun my tires through the thick mud between two hills where a shallow river would run each time it rained, leaving a playground of mud as it dried.

I glanced over at him and chuckled at the wide-eyed look he gave me while he white-knuckled the *oh-shit* handle above his head.

"Don't laugh," he snapped. "And pay attention to what you're doing."

"I know exactly what I'm doing." I swung the truck around, throwing mud in a wide circle as I fishtailed before straightening out again. "We can stop if you want. I didn't realize you were such a chicken."

"A *chicken*? I am *not* a chicken. You are a terrible driver —" he yelped as I hit a small mound of earth before diving into a deeper pit of mud.

My truck was absolutely covered in thick brown gunk, and the windows were spattered with blobs that stubbornly held on through the rough terrain.

"A chicken who yelps like a puppy," I taunted. "Interesting."

"I hate you, Memphis Hale." His lips were pinched together when I glanced over at him.

I sighed. "All right. Let's get out of here before you have a full-on meltdown."

Tristan shook his head. "Nope. Do your worst because I'm not an animal of any kind. And if I was, I'd be a lion. Brave as fuck."

I bit my lip to hide a grin. "You sure?"

He nodded. "Yep. I'd be king of the motherfucking pride."

Fuck, he was weird. Why did I find that so endearing?

"Okay, King Tristan. Let's do this." I floored it, and my truck went flying through the mud. Tristan's other hand shot to my thigh as we approached an incline, fingers gripping my leg tight. Those same fingers were less than an inch from touching my dick. Between the adrenaline from the ride and the pinch of pain from his nails near my cock, my dick thickened in my jeans. I swallowed a groan, and sank my teeth into my lower lip, nearly drawing blood.

The distraction was why I'd temporarily forgotten the other side of the small hill was harder to navigate. I needed to take a certain path to maintain enough traction and speed to make it through the pit.

His fingers dug in through my jeans, my dick throbbed, and I let off the gas. And then nothing. My tires spun as I refocused. But we weren't going anywhere.

Tristan removed his hand and whipped his head around to face me, expression twisted into a scowl. "Are we fucking stuck?"

I grinned as I snatched my phone from the cup holder to dial Bishop. "Afraid so, my king."

SIX

TRISTAN

STRIKE NUMBER ONE. Or five. I wasn't sure anymore. I'm not a fucking baseball player, okay?

I should probably count strike one as Memphis being straight. Strike two, his ego pissed me off. Strike three...well, see strike two again. That's at least worth three strikes.

The last one? I grimaced as I shook another glob of mud from my fingers I'd collected when I opened the truck door. Memphis was a liar.

I glared at him as we stood beside the truck in knee-deep mud, waiting to be rescued from the swamp of nightmares. "I thought you knew what you were doing."

"I do," Memphis swore, not looking up as his fingers flew across the screen of his phone, tapping out a text, letting someone know where we were. "But someone's been out here stirring this shit up. Besides, it's just part of the fun. Most of the time, you conquer the mud. But sometimes it sucks you into its depths, and well, you lose." He stuffed it in his pocket. "Help is on the way."

"Who?" I inquired.

"Bishop. I was going to message Logan, but I'm pretty

sure Colton—his boyfriend—had a thing..." Memphis finally glanced at me and froze. Then a full belly laugh that shook his shoulders took over the idiot.

I scowled. "What the hell is so funny, you fannypack loving asshole?"

Instead of replying, he reached out and ran his thumb over my cheek before flinging a chunk of mud on the ground. "You are fucking covered. How did you manage that?"

"Not the way you're about to." I barely gave him a warning before I shoved his ginormous body back. His shoes got stuck in the sludge, and he fell on his ass.

Of course, he didn't give me the satisfaction of getting mad. Memphis flopped backward, sinking into the brown gunk, officially out of his mind now, and continued to laugh.

"There is something seriously wrong with you," I accused as I stared down at him, trying to pinpoint on what level of crazy he was currently residing.

Memphis propped himself up on his elbows. "It's just a little mud. You telling me you have a problem getting dirty?"

The challenging glint in his dark blue eyes beneath the shadow of his hat made me stiffen and brought a sense of déjà vu from our first conversation. Apparently I still needed to convince him I was fine with getting fucking filthy. "Oh, I can get dirty, but probably not the kind you mean. I'm as dirty as they *come*."

Memphis's nostrils flared, and he opened his mouth before snapping it shut, grinding his jaw.

"Problem?" I flashed a satisfied grin. Ah, to see Memphis squirm. It really was a thing of beauty.

He shook his head and reached for me. "Nope, not at all. Just wanted to test the theory."

His fingers laced with mine, and I gawked at the sight of Memphis holding my hand.

"What are you—" I gasped as I was suddenly yanked down, landing halfway on top of the brute. My other half sank into the same mud that now coated us both. Shocked, I stared at Memphis in horror. Until he winked, making me bristle. I growled and shook my hand free from his rough grasp. Pushing up, I ignored the hard muscle of his chest beneath my palm and narrowed my eyes. "I hate you so much right now. I never should have agreed to this clearly insane idea."

I was sure my hair was caked now, and who knew what my eyeliner looked like.

"You don't hate me." His chest rumbled, deep and rough. "I'm just keeping my promise. There's not a *speck* of mud on you."

I scampered off of him as gracefully as I could while slipping in the mud. "I do. I really do. You are officially the bane of my existence."

"So dramatic." He smirked, and I opened my mouth to snap back.

The sound of an engine rumbling closer cut off my retort, and I looked toward the direction we'd come, just as Bishop's new truck came dawdling down the trail. He drove slower than my grandma, which really took away from his badass appeal. And if he wasn't careful, he was going to end up stuck like us.

Bishop was Rendon's older brother, Shaw's boyfriend. He was also intense and broody, with unruly black hair, midnight black eyes, a cleft chin, and a tall, muscular body. I hadn't seen either Shaw or Bishop for a while. They barely left their house except to work or the two occasions Rendon had visited, and we all got together. I was pretty sure it was because they were constantly banging.

Bishop smartly curled around the hill and came to a stop on the grassy area next to us. He popped open the driver's side door. Then Shaw, a much larger version of Rendon, minus the black glasses, stepped out of the passenger side before two more big bodies slid out from the back. I didn't recognize the last two, but from the look of them, they were definitely two extra football players added to this now jock-crowded mix.

"Hot damn." Memphis whistled. "Tell me that's Rush Jaggers and Torin Hopkins."

I glanced down at Memphis. "Um, who?"

He looked up at me. "Torin was the Saints QB before me. And Rush was his center. Pro now."

My suspicion was confirmed, but Memphis looked way more impressed. I didn't care who they were. I just hoped they could drag us out of there.

All four stopped on the bank, not appearing as keen as Memphis about getting covered in mud. He hadn't even attempted to stand.

Shaw's smooth timbre broke our stare. "Torin, I'd like you to meet your replacement."

Torin swiped his light blond hair away from his forehead, sky blue eyes sparkling, and chuckled. "I recognize him from TV, even though he was a bit cleaner."

"I assure you, this is normal." Bishop's raspy voice always came as a surprise because he rarely spoke unless it was to Shaw. Even as he addressed Torin, his obsidian eyes were glued to his boyfriend. Creepy bastard. "Mostly."

His dark gaze landed on me, and no lie, a cold chill ran across my skin.

"This is all Memphis's fault. I was practically kidnapped and forced into this situation," I explained.

Memphis laughed, and I jerked my head down to properly glare at him. The others paid no attention. *What if I really had been kidnapped?* Assholes.

"I'll grab the chain," said Rush, the giant with short brown hair, as he headed for the bed of the truck, Torin following.

"Dude, what are Rush and Torin doing here?" Memphis whispered to his friends.

Shaw grinned. "You starstruck?"

"Fuck yes." Memphis didn't even bother to hide it either. He stared wide-eyed at the pair lifting a heavy chain that clanked as Rush gathered it.

"How the hell did you get stuck?" Shaw asked.

Memphis snorted. "I was distracted. Someone wouldn't stop running their mouth and griping like a baby."

I stiffened. "A *baby*?"

Shaw chuckled just as the two guys came back.

"Sorry, man. This part's on you," Rush said as he held out one end. Memphis stood and stared at the mess that clung to me, biting his lip in a way that told me he was fighting another laugh. Now once again conscious of how I looked, I scanned the newcomers. They were all hot in their own way. But Memphis, even messy as he was, made my blood heat. I scowled. No, he didn't. Definitely not. My blood was ice cold. Practically frozen, really.

Nodding at myself with satisfaction, I watched as Memphis took the heavy chain, then wrapped and attached it to a front bar on his truck.

As he worked, Shaw spoke to me. "Do I need to ask what you're doing here, Tris? Does Rendon know you're hanging out with Memphis?"

No, he didn't because I hadn't had a chance to talk to him. "I told you I was kidnapped. I haven't had a chance to report it yet."

Shaw grinned like always. I didn't bother to look at the others because I knew none of them believed me anyway.

"Okay, we're ready," Memphis said, and he and Bishop headed for their trucks.

"You may want to move," Rush warned. "This could get messy."

I briefly wondered if the dude had twenty-twenty vision. Because I was already gross.

"DID I change your mind about me?" Memphis asked while pulling into my apartment's parking lot, leaving clumps of mud behind on the pavement.

"Definitely. We can add liar to the list," I snapped. Mud was caked in places it did not belong, and the cab was filled with an earthy scent that wasn't entirely unpleasant. Not that I'd ever admit that to Memphis.

Memphis attempted to hide a grin, but the stupid dimple popped anyway. Not that I noticed. Because I didn't care. "It's not funny."

"It kind of is, actually." He didn't bother to contain his grin any longer, and those dimples...

As soon as he pulled alongside the curb close to my unit, I huffed and slung open the door, muttering, "Your dimples are stupid."

"Really? That's a new one." When I flicked an annoyed glance his way, his brows were high, and a smile twisted his lips.

"Well, they are." I scowled and mumbled under my

breath, "Stupidly distracting." His grin grew, and I bristled. "You have supersonic hearing or something?"

He ignored the question, batting it away with a lazy wave. "Fine. My facial features aside, what do I have to do to change your mind about me?"

I tilted my head and squinted. "Why do you care so much what I think?"

Memphis shrugged. "Answer the question."

"Answer mine first," I volleyed back.

He hesitated. "I don't know."

"See? I told you, you were a liar." I glared.

Memphis laughed, the husky sound making my traitorous body shiver. "How do you know I'm lying?"

"Because you just admitted it." Obviously. Good thing he was hot.

Memphis gave me a pointed look, shrouded by humor. "Being friends with you might be challenging."

"Friends?" My eyebrows shot high. "How did you come to that conclusion? You were ignoring me like five minutes ago."

Memphis shrugged. "And I'm trying to fix it. Just tell me what I have to do to change your mind."

I narrowed my eyes at him, trying to figure out his angle. His expression was earnest enough, but it didn't mean I wasn't confused as hell. Having a hot friend around to ogle might not be completely terrible. I'd eventually figure out why he was suddenly showing interest. I tapped my chin, scowling when it came in contact with drying mud once again. "I don't know. Maybe you could do something I actually like to do."

He didn't hesitate. "Fine. What do you have in mind?"

My grin stretched my cheeks. "How do you feel about sex clubs?"

Memphis coughed and sat up straighter. Clearing his throat, he rasped, "Uh, what?"

I shook my head and gave him a disappointed sigh. "Figures you'd balk at a totally acceptable way to spend a weekend. Well, thanks for today." I waved and took a step back.

"Fine," Memphis growled.

I froze and didn't bother to mask my shock. "Wow, really? Because I was totally kidding." Memphis's cheeks heated, and my lips stretched into a crazed smile because... "Are you blushing?"

"Tristan," Memphis growled. The sound was sexy as fuck. And I could, unfortunately, imagine all too well what it would sound like while he was fucking me. Sometimes I really hated my overactive imagination.

"Chill, big guy. I was only kidding." I shrugged. "There's a club I like to go to on the weekends, and unfortunately, they would kick you out if you started boning in the middle of the establishment. Next Saturday after your game? It's a home game, right?"

"It is. Starts at three." Memphis paused. "I'll pick you up after, and we'll go where you want."

"It's a date—except not a date, of course." My imagination was in full overdrive because his cheeks appeared to deepen in color, if possible. Whatever. I tugged the disgusting fabric of my shirt away from my skin. "I need to go wash this shit off me. Next time I get dirty, I prefer sweat and skin, hard—"

"*Tristan,*" Memphis scolded while rudely interrupting me. Despite his bark, heat flared in his eyes before it disappeared. Or it was yet another fantasy I'd made up. "You are allowed to keep some things to yourself."

"Why would I do that when I can just tell you?" I asked. When Memphis groaned, I bit back a smile. The only redeeming part of the day was watching Memphis's usually confident swagger falter. He'd better believe I'd tap into that as often as possible. I took a step back before shutting the door. As I walked away, I couldn't help but notice the rough rumble of his engine remained idling behind me the entire time it took me to make it inside my apartment. Once inside, I hurried to the blinds and peeked out just as Memphis pulled away.

Friends with a football player? The quarterback, at that? Sometimes I really wished I had more impulse control.

SEVEN

TRISTAN

THE FOLLOWING SATURDAY, I leaned in close to my bathroom mirror, pulling the skin tightly around each eye as I drew slim lines of black eyeliner around them. When I was finished, I leaned back to examine my appearance, hoping to grab Memphis's attention. Apparently, I didn't care that he was straight.

Choosing dark colors, as usual, I decided on a pair of black skinny jeans and a dark blue t-shirt. I'd dressed up my outfit with a silver chain bracelet and a necklace with a cross in the center. My jet-black hair was styled as usual, long on one side and shaved short on the other, and the black eyeliner made my pale blue irises pop. Satisfied, I left the bathroom to grab my wallet when the knock came at the door. Nervous energy coiled in my gut, the feeling foreign after spending so much time focusing on building my confidence back after high school—and honestly, a concrete barrier between other people's opinions and how they affected me. I wasn't sure I liked the new sensation, especially because it gave me hope that Memphis would notice me in a way that was impossible for a straight dude.

Already annoyed with myself, I marched down the hall, crossed the living room, and flung open the door. Memphis stood there, hot as fuck, with his thumbs hooked into the pockets of a pair of dark jeans that hugged his ridiculously muscled legs. The black button-up shirt he wore did nothing to hide the wide expanse of his chest. Thankfully he hadn't really messed with his hair. It still held the freshly-fucked-just-rolled-out-of-bed look, which I quickly realized was worse. I didn't appreciate it because it sent my mind to more places it didn't belong. His gaze ran over me, sending a shiver over my skin.

Clearly, Memphis was determined to fuck with my head. I hadn't seen him since the mudding catastrophe and had only spoken to him twice. The first time, after my drain had gotten clogged, thanks to the mud, and the second when he was on his way to my apartment twenty minutes ago.

Memphis broke the odd staring contest, clearing his throat as he stepped back. "Ready to go?"

I scowled. That was it? After all the ogling I'd offered, and maybe he had too? Rolling my eyes, I huffed out a dramatic breath. Determined to pry a compliment from his lips, I turned completely around to give him a nice view of my ass in my tight jeans and made a show of snatching my keys from the decorative entry table by the door.

Still not a single peep from him. The fuck?

When I spun back around, I could have sworn he was checking me out, but he jerked his head to the side before I could decide if I'd imagined the whole thing.

The truth was my skinny, short frame had nothing on Memphis's body which was a thousand times more appetizing. Still, a little acknowledgment about how great my ass looked wouldn't have killed him. Straight or not, a nice ass was a nice ass.

Still frowning, I tacked on a glare. "Hello to you too, Memphis. You look great too. Also, congrats on the win today."

"Thank you... And you look fine," he said reluctantly, even as his gaze darted up and down my body, lingering on certain places a half-second too long.

My brow rose, and I didn't even bother not attempting to mess with him. "Fine or *fine?*"

Memphis rolled his eyes as he took another step back, jingling his keys in his hand, clearly prompting me to get moving. "You look...good, okay? Stop fishing for compliments."

"*Good,*" I mimicked, noting his lack of enthusiasm as I turned to lock the door and then back around.

I studied him carefully as I said, "Hopefully, there will be some guys there tonight who will appreciate my tight little body and picture bending me over—"

"Tristan!" he snapped, surprisingly cutting me off with a bit more venom than I'd expected. I bit back a laugh at the glare he shot at me. However, I still couldn't determine if he was more annoyed with my extremely inappropriate commentary or if the idea of a guy fucking me was the problem. Which of course didn't make sense.

"Lead the way," I commanded and then followed him downstairs, out to the parking lot where he'd parked his truck. When I hopped into the cab and shut the door, I glanced around the clean interior and sniffed the air filled with the scent of polished leather. "I'm surprised you were able to get all of the mud out of here."

As Memphis cranked the engine, a loud growl filled the

night, vibrating the seat beneath me. "I had to take it to get detailed. It was bad."

"I remember," I scoffed, still not able to completely forgive him.

He chuckled, and the tension between us bled away. Pulling away from the spot, Memphis headed for the highway not too far from my complex.

"You get directions?" I asked. I'd only texted him the name of the club.

He nodded and took the on-ramp toward the busier city that bordered Sugar Land. "Yep. And I searched their website to verify you weren't actually dragging me to a sex club."

"Bummer, right?" I snorted. "I know how much you were secretly looking forward to that."

Memphis shot me a quick glance filled with frustration. "I wasn't actually going to go to a sex club with you, Tristan."

I nodded, although I wasn't convinced that was the truth. He'd agreed to the idea pretty damn fast, which still didn't make a lot of sense. I sang, "Liar, liar, honey sweet-flavored lube's pants on fire."

A growl met my reply. "Whatever. Think what you want, and I'm not even going to touch the *honey...* thing."

Scanning over his muscular build, I grinned. "I am definitely having inappropriate thoughts. Want to hear them?"

He gave an exasperated sigh. "No. And stop staring at me."

"You literally just said to think what I want," I pointed out.

"That's not what I meant." Memphis shifted in his seat, squirming, which of course, brought a maniacal grin to my lips.

I shrugged and glanced out the window. "Next time, be more specific."

Memphis cleared his throat. "So, this club we are going to is your weekend spot?"

"Not really," I replied as I watched the darkened sky lit by a full moon. Bishop's dad owned a club close to where we were heading, a snazzy one too. Still, everyone who knew the broody bastard had collectively decided it was off-limits. Fine by me. I didn't support assholes. I glanced back at Memphis. "But sometimes when I want to..."

He waited, but I remained mute just to irritate him. "Don't leave me hanging. When you want to what?"

Memphis had one large hand lazily wrapped around the wheel. Cool and calm again. Time to stir that up. "When I want to fuck."

He stiffened, and his chiseled jaw clenched tight.

My brows shot high at the unexpected reaction. "You cool, big guy?"

Slowly his body melted back into his relaxed posture, and I scanned him head to toe. Or at least what I could see of him. What the fuck was up with him?

Memphis shrugged, almost appearing unaffected. Hell, maybe he was, and again, it was probably more about my lack of tact than the idea of other guys. Yeah, probably that.

"Yeah, I'm good. So, you meet guys here?" Memphis prodded as he watched the road.

"Sometimes. I mean, it's not a gay club, but I use this app thing and get lucky sometimes." He stiffened again, causing me to really study his whiplash postures. "You having some sort of spasm attack or something?"

Once again, he relaxed and shot me an irritated look before staring ahead again. "You use a hookup app?"

"Of course, I do. Don't tell me you don't." Almost the

entire student body used it simply for convenience. "And I swear if you lock up again, we are going to go to the hospital instead of the club."

Memphis's odd behavior was sending warning signals pulsing in my brain, but I wasn't quite sure what the warning was about.

His hand tightened and closed around the wheel. "Like you said. Of course, I do."

Bitter jealousy, a feeling I hadn't really known until this second, rose up hot and swift. I was the one that tensed this time. More so when Memphis glanced at me and quirked his lips. "You okay there, emo guy?"

Crossing my arms over my chest, I scowled. "Whatever's wrong with you must be contagious." Memphis snorted, the sound all wrong coming from the big dumb sexy jock. Yet, oddly, it made me go all soft inside. "Did you seriously just snort?"

It was his turn to scoff. "Definitely did not."

"Sure you didn't." I pointed at the upcoming exit that flowed into the bustling downtown area that glowed from the bright lights of restaurants, clubs, tattoo parlors, and eclectic shops. "Take this one."

Memphis flipped on his blinker. "I said I know where we're going, Tris."

Tris? When had I gained a nickname? Not even Rendon called me that. Why did I like it so much?

I frowned. Memphis was annoying. Not endearing. At all. So I did *not* like it.

I was so distracted pondering this new development, I barely registered driving down the busy street or pulling into the parking lot of the two-story club. When Memphis popped open his door, he shook me from my thoughts, and I unlatched my seatbelt. When I slid down from the lifted beast, I found him waiting in front of the truck, eyeing me with humor dancing in his dark blue eyes. "Do I need to get you a step stool?"

I glared. "Do I need to get you a..."

Memphis eyed me expectantly, but I had nothing. Blank. Zero comebacks. *Was I broken?*

His lips twitched, and my gaze narrowed further. "Shut up, you big elf goblin."

"I thought elves were small," he replied like a know-it-all.

Ignoring him again, I stomped off toward the long line of scantily clad girls and guys waiting to get inside, the latter of whom I would normally have considered attractive if I didn't have a frustratingly hot football player trailing my steps. Unfortunately, the sound of a husky chuckle behind me had my undivided attention.

"Dick pirate," I mumbled.

"That makes zero sense, as usual." His voice was louder than I expected, and I was startled when he appeared at my side. "Where do you come up with that shit, anyway?"

I considered ignoring him, simply because I was mad he'd snuck up on me. But he was my best friend now after all, and Rendon knew my secret. I spilled. "I found a generator online to help me out."

Memphis snorted. "I'm a little disappointed. I thought for sure you came up with that crazy stuff on your own."

"Hey!" I frowned. "I put my own spin on them, thank you."

"Impressive." Memphis did not sound impressed at all.

Now I really was going to ignore him. Probably. That lasted a full thirty seconds because his long strides caused me to damn near jog to keep up. Since I didn't have an athletic bone in my body, it was uncomfortable. "It's rude to walk so fast beside someone with shorter legs."

"It looks stupid for me to take small baby steps," he countered but slowed his steps anyway. "So, this app you use... Are you planning to use it tonight?"

This shift in topics was so extreme, it took me a moment to process the question. I hadn't really considered logging into the app, but Memphis didn't need to know that. "Dunno. Maybe. Guess it depends if I get horny." *For someone other than you*, I tacked on mentally. Though that wasn't even a remote possibility.

He glared at me this time. "You better not ditch me."

"Like you wouldn't find someone easily enough." And it was true. Memphis was dead sexy. Didn't matter if he was sweaty in his uniform or dressed to torture me for a night out, he could have his pick from many of the girls who were openly staring at him. My glare shifted to them. *Hands and eyes off my non-date, ladies.*

Our conversation was cut short as we joined the line and waited for our turn to be let inside. After a fifteen-minute wait, we showed our IDs, paid the entry fee, and stepped through the club door.

Inside we were immediately engulfed in the loud bass that vibrated the floors and walls around us. The warehouse-type building was packed tonight with bodies writhing on the dance floor beneath the glow of constant gradient shifts of purple to blue light streaming from the rafters. Tables crowded around the perimeter were overflowing with people laughing, taking shots, or sipping on beers.

"You want a drink?" Memphis asked close to my ear.

I turned and nearly brushed his lips with mine. We both jerked back at the same time, yet I was immediately offended. My lips were almost as great as my ass. *Dick.* "Can't. You're already twenty-one?"

His throat bobbed as he stared over my shoulder. Was he avoiding looking at me, or had someone already caught his attention? "Oh, right. Yep, birthday was last month."

Well, at least he remembered he was speaking to me. I brushed off the irritation. Memphis was straight and single. I should have been prepared for what that meant when going to a club. Hell, I thought I had. "You dance, right?"

He smirked, making one stupid dimple pop. "Maybe."

I scanned his body as if I didn't already have it memorized. He was probably telling the truth because, of course, he had to be amazing at everything. Still, I would have to see it to believe it. "I need a water."

We began heading toward the long bar without a word as we dodged people and wove our way through the crowd.

Ten minutes later, drinks in hand, we stood against a wall like a pair of losers, watching everyone around us having a blast.

I took a large swallow from my water bottle and then twisted the cap back on, shouting over the noise, "I thought you said you could dance!"

Memphis tilted his head to stare down at me. "I said I could. *Not* that I would."

"You came to a club, not to dance?" I eyed him closely. Maybe he'd lied about owning some actual moves. "You can't really dance, can you?"

He leaned down close to my ear. "You calling me a liar again?"

I nodded emphatically. "That is correct."

"I don't see you out there shaking your ass," he challenged, and I rolled my eyes. I definitely had skills on the dance floor.

"Whatever. I promised this annoying guy I wouldn't ditch him. And unless I use my app, I'm not going to know which guys are into it." At the mention of the app, Memphis stiffened again. He had issues with the app, I realized, but I didn't know why, especially since he used one himself. Nash had worried about Rendon using the same one—or that was his excuse anyway. Maybe Memphis was concerned about me because I was admittedly petite. "I'm not trying to grind on a straight dude and get my ass kicked, thank you very much. And I still don't believe you. In fact, I dare you to show me what you got."

He thrust his water out toward me, and I caught it just as he let go. "Sure."

Sure? Before I could voice the question, Memphis was stalking out onto the floor. I swear it took maybe two seconds for a curvy brunette to smile, turn, and rub her barely-covered ass on his junk. His long fingers curled around her wide hips, and then... yeah, okay, Memphis could dance. But that was *not* what I meant. In my rash decision to call him out, a corner of my mind had thought it would be with me, which made no sense. Still pissed me off.

I eyed the pair, dancing closer than necessary. Memphis wasn't exactly stopping her from grinding against his dick. Encouraged it, really. But he didn't seem to really register the girl. Even though he was moving to the beat, touching her, he stared at me, lifting a brow as if to say, *see?*

I downed my water as I glared at them.

"Too sexy for his own good jerk off banana," I muttered as I turned away, completely over the scene. After depositing both of our drinks on the nearest table, I retreated into the shadows and slipped my phone from my pocket. If he was going to dance with a girl, I would find my own entertainment. Just because I called him out didn't mean he actually had to rise to the challenge. I huffed as I pulled up my app, only to have my phone snatched from my hands before I could even press another button.

"The hell?" I seethed and glanced up at the unexpected big body looming over me.

Memphis checked the screen and frowned. "Decided to use it after all, huh?"

I snatched it back from him and shoved it into my pocket before crossing my arms over my chest. "You seemed a bit busy. Didn't think you'd mind."

Silently, he stared down at me before shaking his head, sending his messy brown hair fluttering down his forehead. "You told me to go dance. No, you dared me."

There was no way I was admitting that I had hoped he'd prove that he could dance *with me.* "And? I'm not complaining. I was just attempting to find someone to hang out with."

"Hang out with *or fuck?*" His lips curled in... anger? Disappointment?

I shrugged. "Does it matter?"

"You said you wouldn't ditch me. You actually told me that like two minutes ago." A vee formed between his eyebrows, and his intense stare held mine steady.

I poked a finger into his chest. "And again, you seemed preoccupied."

He grabbed my hand, preventing another stab into his thick muscles. But he didn't let go. "And again, you told me to."

For fucks sake, we were just going around in circles, and the argument was only growing louder. "I can do this all night. I can do a lot of things all night. Why don't you go find that girl and leave me to it?"

I went for my phone again, and Memphis slammed his hand against the wall over my shoulder. He leaned down, dipping close so that his lips hovered in front of mine, only mere inches separating us. He stood still, frozen, as his breaths raced in and out of his lungs, coasting over my lips in a way that made them tingle. He was so close, the minty scent filled my nose. All I had to do was lean forward the tiniest bit, and I'd be kissing his stupidly perfect mouth. I wondered how he'd react.

His nostrils flared, and then without a word, he tore himself away with a curse, taking several steps back and scrubbed a hand over his face. "You want to get on your app and find some guy to take you home? Fine. I think I'm going to head out, though."

"With that girl?" I snapped, straightening from the wall.

Memphis watched me closely with a clenched jaw. "No."

One word. No explanation. "Why? I'm sure she'd be down."

"Because I don't want to, Tristan," he practically growled before he seemed to force himself to relax. Even if it was barely noticeable.

"You certain about that?" I glanced down at the large bulge in his jeans. "Your dick is hard."

Memphis shamelessly reached down and rearranged his junk. "I'm seriously fucking sure I don't want to take *her* home."

Jesus, he was as moody as Bishop. Had she done something to piss him off?

I guess that meant we were both leaving because Memphis's cock was now on my mind, and there was zero interest in anyone else at the moment. It should have pissed me off. I had no business thinking about his dick—no more than I already did. But I was currently suffering from blood loss to the brain because it was uncomfortably taking up space in my already too-tight pants. What a waste of a night and the hour it had taken me to get ready.

Fan-fucking-tastic. I scowled. "Let's go then. I need to jerk off."

Memphis choked on nothing but air. Impressive. Guess he did have a flaw if simply breathing was an issue.

EIGHT

MEMPHIS

AFTER A GRUELING TWO hours on the practice field, the hot water from the locker room shower felt amazing, beating down on my skin. But I knew the reprieve would be short-lived.

Visiting my parents was the last thing I wanted to do after a full day of classes and football. Especially since my mind was still on Saturday night. On Tristan specifically.

I really wasn't sure what drew me to the smart-mouthed guy. He was nothing like the boy with red puffy eyes I'd found beneath that tree when we'd met. Now Tristan was bright and bold—intriguing in a completely different way. That night I couldn't stop myself from placing a soft kiss on his tear-stained lips. And Saturday, I'd almost done it again. Except this time, the desire to kiss him had been born from need that bordered on irrational violence. Just the thought of him hooking up with another guy had pissed me off and caught me completely off guard.

Of course, I hadn't come clean to Tristan about why my dick had gotten hard from almost stupidly kissing him. He had no idea that girl had nothing to do with my cock being damn near ready to rip open my zipper.

I'd wanted to press him against the wall, grab his tight little ass, and grind my dick against his. The photo of his cock with the Prince Albert piercing—a shiny metal ring through the tip—had catapulted into my memory and driven me mad.

Even now, my dick plumped at the image—the last thing I needed to have in an open shower full of my teammates.

I wanted Tristan. But I couldn't do a damn thing about it. Not without spilling my secret or without telling him we had a past.

How could I be around him all the time without telling him the truth? How was I supposed to keep my lips off his when all I wanted was to bury my tongue down his throat?

Angry at myself, I flipped the shower off and snagged my towel, quickly tying it around my waist while attempting to hide the bulge with my hand.

"Where are you off to in such a hurry?" Logan asked as he trailed me to our lockers.

I popped mine open and scrubbed myself dry harder than necessary. Between the feel of the rough terrycloth and Logan's voice, my semi deflated, so I dropped the towel and grabbed my boxer briefs. "Have to be at my parents' for an early dinner, and I'm running late."

"Damn, that sucks. I know they aren't your favorite people." Logan dressed beside me as I tugged on my jeans and pulled my shirt over my head.

He was right. They weren't. The pressure my parents had put on me about going pro was almost enough to make me walk away from the sport. But the game was coded in my DNA, and I couldn't do it. "I'll survive."

"Everything good?" Logan asked and raised a brow when I glanced at him. "You were off your game today."

He was right. My passes had been absolute shit and my timing embarrassingly off. My world was a chaotic mess at the moment because I'd invited Tristan into my life. And now I was stuck with the consequences of hiding shit from him. I was an asshole, but what the hell was I supposed to do? Tell him the truth and risk him walking away? That would probably be best, but I couldn't do it. I liked having him around, and I was fully aware I was a selfish bastard. Looking away, I grabbed my shoes and yanked them on my feet. "Yeah, it's all good. I just have a lot on my mind."

Fuckin' truth.

He nodded. "You ever need an ear..."

"Thanks, man, but I'm okay." I stood, shoved my sweaty clothes in my gym bag, grabbed my hat, and slid it on backward before gathering my other things. Glancing at the time on my phone, I cursed and slung my bag over my shoulder. "I gotta go, or my parents are going to throw a fit."

"Okay. Colt is probably outside waiting, so I have to get my ass moving too. See ya in the morning," Logan replied.

"Bright and early." I saluted him while saying my goodbyes to the other guys before pushing through the door into the practice facility.

The building was empty except for the tanned guy with sun-kissed blond hair. Colt.

"He on his way out?" Colt asked and glanced at the locker room door. I still had a hard time wrapping my head around the whole Logan has a boyfriend, and the girlfriend had been an elaborate ruse. They seemed happy though, so I was glad for them.

I nodded to him as I continued on, calling back, "Yeah, he should be."

The evening air was still sticky from the humidity and a stark contrast to the weather from only a week ago. I missed the cold as I crossed the parking lot to my truck.

My phone rang as soon as I hit the highway toward my parents' house. The radio display showed Nash was calling. Due to our busy schedules, I hadn't talked to him since the day Tristan had unknowingly found me on the app. I didn't need that mental image again, so I hit answer.

"What's up?"

"Shaw says you took Tristan out," Nash blurted, jumping straight to the point.

I shouldn't have been surprised he knew. It could have been any one of the guys that had helped us out of the mud, but it made sense Shaw would have run his mouth. Maybe Tristan had filled Rendon in on the club, and he would have shared the details with Nash and Shaw.

Still, I hadn't expected the blunt comment. I paused for a second and finally responded, "The club?"

"What club? You took him to a club, too?" Nash was clearly surprised, and it became instantly apparent I'd been wrong. Tristan hadn't spilled to Rendon. Well fuck. Nash continued, "I was talking about the mudding trip you took your little emo on."

"Shut up. Tristan isn't mine, and I didn't take him out." Not the way he meant anyway. Sort of. Or at least it hadn't started that way. Hell, I wasn't even sure how it ended.

Nash growled. "What are you doing, Memphis?"

"Nothing, damn." I glared at the screen even though he couldn't see me. "It's not like what you're implying. We're... just friends. So, we've hung out a few times. What's the big deal?"

Nash chuckled, more disbelief bleeding in his tone

when he responded, "You know he had a boner for you all last year, right?"

Having watched him, despite trying not to, I had noticed Tristan looking at me—often—but I dodged the question. "It's seriously not like that. I saw him at the party, and he sort of went off on me." A small grin spread across my lips, and I immediately squashed it, knowing Nash would hear it in my voice. "I don't know why I did it, but I just sort of invited him."

I didn't tell Nash how Tristan had unknowingly messaged me, intending to fuck a perfect stranger. At least as far as he knew. And I definitely wasn't going to admit I had a photo of Tristan's dick on my phone because I'd stupidly responded to his message, requesting a picture.

"So, what's the deal now?" Nash continued to dig into my business.

"Like I said, we're friends. *Just* friends." For once, the exit leading to my parents' house was a welcome sight. "I'm almost to Palace Hale. I have to go."

"Whatever you say, man. But for Rendon's sake, I have to warn you to be careful with Tristan. You say you're just friends, but he has a thing for you, plain and simple. Don't hurt him," Nash warned.

"Loud and clear. Later, Dad." I disconnected before he could respond. Nash was probably right to warn me, but he didn't know that it was too late for me to back out. At this point, I wasn't a hundred percent sure I wouldn't get burned a little in the aftermath of coming clean, and that was unexpected. When Tristan found out the truth... I didn't know how he'd react, and it was just dawning on me that I wouldn't have a choice. I would have to tell him eventually. I just didn't know how or when.

The relief I'd felt from the excuse of arriving at my

parents' vanished as soon as I turned into their ridiculously long, wide driveway. Obscuring the front door stood a porte-cochere protruding from the three-story house. The structure had been "a must" during the new build so their wealthy friends and clients could enter the house without braving the rain or sun.

My parents' house wasn't absurdly extravagant. Not like Bishop's dad's anyway, but in my opinion, it was still too much for just the two of them. The red brick was accented with blinding white trim outlining the tall gables, and manicured shrubbery made the house appear flawless, almost fabricated. It made me wish I'd taken my truck through another river of mud before I'd come over. My lips twitched as I thought of how incongruous my muddy truck would look in front of all this. Not to mention how my parents absolutely hated my refusal to drive a brand-new model that would blend with their lifestyle. No thanks. That wasn't me and never would be. The fact they paid for my education rubbed me the wrong way because it gave them the impression they had the right to run the rest of my life. I wanted my own money. Money I earned, but my schedule and rules prevented me from doing that.

Resigned, I slid out of my truck, then climbed the broad white stairs. Not bothering to ring the doorbell, I stepped through the front door and removed my shoes to avoid tracking dirt through the house. Even though I knew what I would find, I glanced to the right, where an enormous stone fireplace loomed over the large den. The dark-stained mantle showcased a row of trophies and framed pictures of me, all of them in my football uniforms. Saints décor was everywhere. Even the guest bathroom was totally decorated in black and gold. Obsessed didn't begin to describe my parents' interest in my budding career.

Shaking my head, I followed the sounds of clanging pots and pans as I strode toward the kitchen. Dark hardwood floors were laid all throughout the house except for the bedrooms. I could smell the scent of lavender my mother insisted on using to excess mixed with heavy spices and herbs from whatever she was cooking.

When I turned the corner, I found my mom, wearing her usual Saints fan shirt, dicing tomatoes next to the stainless-steel stove that heated a pot of pasta.

At the sound of my footsteps, she glanced at me with a raised brow. "Late practice?"

I wasn't surprised at the cool greeting that spoke volumes about our relationship. "Yeah. Coach wasn't fucking around."

"Language," she hissed before turning with her palms full of the vegetable or fruit—whatever the fuck it was—and tossed them into a bowl of leafy greens. "Your father is in his office. Would you tell him dinner will be ready in five?"

As she moved on, slicing a cucumber, I spun around and braced myself for the barrage of commentary over my game as I headed down the hall to my father's study.

When I walked up, my father was on the phone with his head bent over some paperwork. He wrote quickly, nodding as he listened to whoever was on the other line. "Thanks, I'll give him a call. He'll be ready to sell soon?" His lips quirked into a grin. "Great. I'll set something up this week."

I leaned against the door frame, and his navy-blue eyes lifted up to mine as he hung up the phone. A look of arrogant pride crossed his face as he swept his dark brown hair aside and leaned back in his chair. "How's my star quarterback son doing today?"

Biting back a groan, I offered the best smile I could

muster. I didn't understand why I couldn't just be his son. Why was the sparkle in his eyes always accompanied by the feeling he wouldn't be as proud of me if I quit football? "I'm fine, Dad. Mom said dinner will be ready in a few minutes."

I stepped back to walk away, but he snapped his fingers. "Just a minute, Memphis."

Pausing, I lifted my brow.

He gestured toward the chair that sat in front of his desk, and I held back a sigh as I circled around it and plopped down into the cushy leather. "What's up?" I asked.

"I want to know how everything's going at school." He barely took a breath before moving on to the real reason he wanted to talk. "You have scouts visiting soon."

He didn't want to know about school. He wanted to talk about football. Shocker. But at least he'd tried to give a shit for half a second. That was more than usual.

Since I'd refused to join my parents' company in real estate, he'd been after me about going pro. The Hales were successful. That's just how it was, and if I wasn't, well, I wasn't sure how either of them would take it. I really wasn't sure I even cared. Busting my ass on the field wasn't for them—it was for me.

"Everything's fine. We won our game Saturday," I said needlessly. They would have watched it and critiqued my every move, broke down each play to make a list of unwelcomed suggestions on how to improve my performance. I held the knowledge of the weekly pending critique in the back of my mind through every game, and I hated it.

He nodded. "I know. We watched the game on TV."

I waited silently, knowing he was nowhere near finished.

"The pass to Garret was a mistake. You didn't see Donnelly downfield? Scouts are going to notice those things," he informed me as if I wasn't already fully aware of what the scouts would be taking notes on.

I clenched my fists. "Garret made a thirty-yard run from that play."

"And Donnelly was wide open," he repeated.

He hadn't been. One of the best safeties in the conference had been charging after him, and Donnelly wasn't fast enough to have gotten free and scored on that play. Not to mention his tendency to fumble under pressure would have made that a risky pass, which was why I preferred connecting with Garret in that situation. He had skills and a tighter grip. At that moment, it had been the wisest choice and one that had paid off too. Still, arguing with my dad about it wasn't worth the headache.

I simply nodded, keeping my thoughts to myself. "When we watch the film tomorrow, I'll be sure to look for it."

He nodded, satisfied, as he rose from his seat. "Good. Now, let's go eat before your mother comes looking for us."

Pushing to my feet, I followed him down the hall and back into the kitchen. My mom had already plated our food and placed it at the long table. The sparkling water I loathed sat next to each setting, and a bowl of salad was displayed in the center.

I took my place across from my mom as my dad claimed the head of the six-person table. Again, just another example of the larger than necessary possessions.

We dug into the meal quietly, but I knew the silence wouldn't last. Halfway through my pasta, my mother asked, "So, how is school going?"

"It's going well." I set down my fork, steeling myself for the same questions I fielded twice a month at these gatherings.

She hummed. "Special girl in your life?"

What she really wanted to know was if I was wasting time dating, a distraction they felt was important to avoid so I could focus on my *real* goals.

"No, Mom." I offered a tight smile in a familiar attempt to not stir the pot with a useless argument. I hadn't met anyone I wanted to date anyway. But if I had, I'd be dating, regardless of their opinion.

She smiled in approval, and my dad nodded as he chewed. So ridiculous. Many of the guys had girlfriends, and some even had boyfriends. Their draft prospects were just as promising as mine were, but that wasn't enough for my parents. They were gunning for the number one draft pick.

My mother changed the subject after sipping from her glass. "This weekend, we are showing the house in Greenford to a couple moving from the East Coast."

Grateful for the change of topic, I picked my fork up again. "That's nice."

"It is," she agreed. "That house has sat vacant for too long. Unfortunately, we will be out of town, so we need you to show it instead."

She could have just started with that. It was nothing new. In fact, I had shown and sold half the houses they had renovated and flipped. But I still spent as little of the money they transferred to my bank account as possible even though I earned the cash. They put so much pressure on me over football that I'd considered quitting the game several times, but I wouldn't allow that to happen. Football was my life. I never wanted to feel like I owed them anything or that I was obligated to make decisions that met their standards. I had zero use for that kind of money anyway and planned to donate every last bit of it the second my life was completely my own.

My parents weren't all bad. Sure, they were demanding and overstepped way over the line, but I'd had a good childhood. I really didn't have a reason to rock the boat since they were pushing for something I wanted anyway.

Our conversation grew stilted. We didn't have dialogue that flowed easily but rather felt like an uncomfortable business meeting with strangers. When I finished my dinner, I carried my plate to the sink, planning to make my escape.

I pulled my keys from my pocket and glanced over at both of them still seated at the table. "I need to get going."

"So soon?" My dad's brow furrowed. "I thought we could talk about this weekend's game. I had a few suggestions."

Of course he did. I shrugged and gave an apologetic smile before adding, "I have plans with the guys from the team."

That was a bold-faced lie. I had exactly zero plans with them. And I didn't feel the slightest twinge of guilt for lying about it.

My mom sighed. "We won't see you next weekend, but I'll give you a call about the Jenkins'. That's the couple who'll be looking at the house."

"Sounds good," I murmured while making a round of short goodbyes before heading for the door. The second I stepped onto the porch I took a deep inhale of the muggy air. Fuck, I hated these visits.

Once I was settled into the truck, I checked my phone and saw a missed text. I hadn't even heard my phone ding. I swiped the screen, and my lips twitched at the message.

Tristan: *I'm bored. Unbore me.*

Me: *It's a school night and late. Can't you just go to sleep?*

Tristan: *Late? It's like five o'clock, you lame soccer mom. And as my 'friend', it's your job to fix it. Last year I would have bugged Rendon to get food or something, but now I'm just stuck with you.*

A laugh rumbled from my chest as I tapped on the screen.

Me: *And now that he's gone, you want me to go get food?*

The response was immediate.

Tristan: **Long suffering sigh* Never mind*

I frowned. What did he mean by *never mind?* As was my MO with Tristan, I responded without really thinking it through.

Me: *Where did you want to go?*

Tristan: *Burger and fries. I'm not picky. But like I said, never mind.*

I shook my head, already hearing the ridiculous statement in my head as if he was right next to me. There was no way I could handle another bite of any kind of food, but I still responded back to him.

Me: *I could eat.*

Tristan: *Fine, since you're going to bully me into it.*

A broad grin stretched across my lips. How could he be so exasperatingly weird, and completely... addictive at the same time?

Me: *How long do you need to get ready?*

Tristan: *I'm already ready.*

My shoulders shook with laughter. Of course he was. Maybe I really was that transparent in my inability to stay the fuck away from him. That was probably bad, but after the night I'd had, I almost needed to see Tristan.

Me: *I'm on my way.*

Tristan: *My stomach thanks you.*

NINE
TRISTAN

MEMPHIS HAD CHOSEN to drive us to a burger joint close to my apartment rather than hitting the sandwich shop near campus, likely because I claimed starvation.

My stomach growled as we were seated in a booth at the cozy mom-and-pop restaurant. The crimson-colored walls were decorated with retro posters, the tables covered with red and white gingham tablecloths, and an old jukebox sat in the corner playing old rock songs. The delectable scent of greasy meat, spices, and fresh-baked bread was not helping the situation.

When I'd texted Memphis, I'd counted on him being starved, too, since his body had to burn fifty million calories a day just to function. And honestly, I hadn't wanted to sit alone again. Not because I minded it, but the view of the muscular athlete sitting across from me was so much better. Plus, we were friends now, thanks to his badgering me about it, so it was his job to go with me anyway.

"Eyes up here," Memphis scolded with laughter in his voice.

My head jerked back, tearing my wandering gaze from

the wide expanse of his chest muscles displayed through his gray t-shirt. The curled bill of his ball cap cast shadows over half of his face, making it hard for me to read his expression. Well, except for the amused tip of his lips that creased the dimples in his cheeks. I glared at him. "My eyes are just fine. Your big ass body is blocking my view."

"Yeah? Something behind me catch your attention?" he asked, clearly not believing me. It was irrelevant that he was right. Memphis didn't need to know that, and he definitely didn't need a boost to his already overinflated ego.

Leaning to the side to look around him, I glanced back at him and wiggled my brows. "Maybe."

Memphis scowled, and he glanced over his shoulder toward the row of empty tables. Idiot.

When he faced me again, the cocky jerk's smile slipped back into place. "There is literally no one back there, Tris."

Curious how he'd react if I kept pushing his buttons, I shrugged. "Maybe they just left."

This time he glanced at the door so fast I was pretty sure I heard his neck crack.

When he whipped back around to face me, he scowled, and I bit my lip to keep from smiling. I feigned nonchalance, though honestly, I wasn't sure why he was so pissy about me checking out guys. "Something wrong?"

Memphis leaned back in his seat and just stared at me, one arm resting over the top of the booth while his fingers drummed an irritated rhythm. "You're fucking with me."

"Duh. What do you care anyway?" I slid my napkin in front of me, turning it in circles as I watched him carefully.

"I don't," he insisted with a shrug. "I just don't want a repeat of you trying to ditch me for some random guy again."

I guess that made sense, but it was his fault I'd even

thought about hooking up with someone at the club in the first place. "You could have taken that girl home, you know?"

Memphis flipped his cap backward, giving me a clear view of his stupidly perfect face. His dark eyebrows drew together as he frowned, sitting forward again. "Maybe—but I didn't want to."

Maybe my ass. Annoyed for absolutely no reason because I obviously didn't care who Memphis fucked, I tore at the napkin, spreading bits of wadded-up paper all over the table. "Could have fooled me."

"Why do you sound mad?" Memphis whipped his hand on top of mine, rescuing what was left of the napkin to his side of the table.

At his touch, my fingers tingled like the greedy-for-more jerks they were, just from the simple brush of his calloused palm over my softer flesh.

I frowned, not appreciating the way he called me out or his rudeness. It was my napkin to torture as I saw fit. "I'm not mad. I'm hungry."

"Oh." His lips twitched again. "My bad."

At least he could admit when he was wrong. Because he was. Satisfied with his humble wrongness, I nodded and swept my hair away from my eyes. "Yes. Absolutely. Totally. No idea what you're talking about. At all."

"Obviously." Memphis's dark blue eyes twinkled like twilight on a star-filled night. The fuck? I mentally slapped myself for the stupid thought and because I just realized he didn't believe me again.

My eyes narrowed, but right before I opened my mouth to tear into him, a cheerful voice interrupted me.

"Here ya go, boys." We both whipped around to face the smiling blond waitress at the same time. I hadn't even noticed her approaching. She slid plates of burgers and fries in front of us and stepped back, wiping her hands on the white apron covering her black uniform. "I'll be back to check on you soon."

"Thanks," we both muttered. After she walked away, Memphis picked up a crisp fry while I gripped the loaded burger with both hands, shoving as much in my mouth as possible. I moaned as the smoked flavor burst on my tongue. "Fuck, that's good."

I glanced at Memphis and found him staring at me with the fry suspended halfway to his mouth. His throat bobbed, and he blinked, slightly shaking his head.

Did I have something on my face? "What's up?" I asked.

He cleared his throat. "Nothing. Just super impressed at how much you can fit in your mouth." I swear his cheeks immediately flamed red, convincing me Memphis *was* in fact a blusher. "I meant you don't exactly look like you eat a lot."

"Naturally high metabolism. I do eat a lot." I paused. "And you'd be amazed at how much I can fit in my mouth."

His jaw clenched as he shifted in on the bench. "I didn't need to know that, Tris."

"Hey, I was just clarifying your observation. You really should see what I can do with a dick in my—"

"Tristan," Memphis hissed as he shifted once again. "Shut up."

Rolling my eyes, I took another bite. He didn't want details? Fine by me, but now I was just thinking about his cock and how long and thick it would be, how it would taste —and whether I could deep throat him. Too bad neither of us would ever find out how much I could take because I wasn't lying. I was gifted in the art of sucking dick.

Memphis groaned. "I said *shut up*."

Puzzled, I frowned. "Uh... I didn't say anything."

His molars ground together. "Yes, you did. *Gifted... with...* You know what you said."

What? I thought back over what I could have possibly said. "Sucking dick? Did I say that out loud?"

"Unfortunately," Memphis mumbled before dipping his gaze to the food he'd barely touched.

"Well, it's true," I replied, defending myself because natural talent should be recognized and celebrated. Honestly, there should be a parade for the skill.

Memphis shook his head as he scooped up another fry. "Do you even have a filter? Like at all?"

"Other than the one on my air conditioner, that would be a no. I broke it while sucking—"

Nostrils flaring, his hand slammed against the table. But he still hadn't looked up. "I get it, okay?"

I burst out laughing. "Now *you* sound mad."

"I'm not," he insisted. "I'm just trying to understand your brain, and it's giving me a headache."

"What's wrong with my brain?" I snapped.

"You clearly need to get laid," he muttered and stuffed the fry in his mouth.

"Yeah, about that. I tried, and this football player got his tight boxers in a twist." I wasn't sure what underwear Memphis wore, but I was almost positive he was a boxer-brief guy. My kryptonite. Well, besides dimples.

He frowned. "Because we'd agreed—"

"Round and round in circles we go," I sang, interrupting the cycle.

Memphis was quiet, and for once, I was grateful as we ate in silence. The only thing overpowering my need to further ruffle his feathers and push the limits was that my burger was getting cold.

Once I'd swallowed the last bite, I patted my stomach.

"The quickest way into my pants is to feed me first, you know?"

Memphis choked on the water he'd been drinking before clearing his throat. "I don't want in your pants."

"I didn't say you," I pointed out, but his denial had been so fast I was insulted. "But since we're now best friends, I was just revealing a deeper part of myself. A *lot* deeper. And tight—"

Memphis swore under his breath. "Do not finish that sentence. Friends don't need to know everything about each other."

I huffed. "Fine. But Rendon would let me say whatever I wanted without throwing a fit."

Disappointed by my lackluster new friendship, I slid from the booth. "You ready?" Memphis remained seated, staring at the table. I waited. Still nothing. "Well? Let's go."

He scrubbed a hand over his face. "Give me a minute."

"Yeah, okay." I cocked a brow, wondering what his deal was. "If you aren't ready to part ways, rest assured I have nothing planned tonight. I'm *all* yours."

I wasn't sure why I said stuff just to rile Memphis up, but I couldn't seem to stop myself.

"Trust me, that's not the problem." He swiftly slid out of the booth, and I couldn't help but glance down. The outline of his dick ran down his leg, more visible than usual, and holy shit, it would be a challenge to deep throat that fucker. A challenge I'd gladly accept. *No.* No, I wouldn't, I quickly reminded myself. I didn't fuck egotistical football players. Probably. But why was he sporting a semi anyway? "Let's just go." Memphis didn't say another word as he slapped cash onto the table and then strode toward the front door.

Rude. But I followed behind him anyway.

"Want me to drop you off at your apartment?" he asked once we were in the truck.

I glanced at the clock. It was still fairly early in the evening, and I was caught up on assignments. "What are you doing for the rest of the day?"

Memphis started the truck. "Early night, I guess. I have practice in the morning."

"Seriously? The sun is literally still up." My eyes widened. I'd already gotten the impression that Memphis was more of a homebody than I'd realized, but that was a little ridiculous.

He let out a resigned sigh. "Fine. Tristan, would you like to bug the ever-loving shit out of me for a little bit longer?"

I grinned and buckled my seatbelt. "I'd love to."

"Wanna play in the mud again?" he asked with a flat tone, but he had to be joking.

I scoffed. "Hard pass."

"You sure?" His tone betrayed his amusement.

"Can't we just like...go see a movie or something where I don't need five showers afterward? What would you be doing if you weren't with me?"

He shrugged. "Hanging out at my place. Working out. Sometimes I hang out with Shaw and Bishop. But I'm down for a movie."

"Sweet." I relaxed back into the seat. "Question. Have you ever fucked around in the theater?"

Memphis shook his head as he pulled out of the parking space. "I'm not answering that."

That was a yes. And for some reason, something swirled around in my gut that felt like jealousy. Probably just indigestion, though, because again, Memphis could crawl into as many pairs of panties as he wanted. Not my business. Because I gave zero fucks. None.

Memphis

DISTRACTED by everything Tristan had decided to over-share at the restaurant, I barely registered the drive to the movie theater. Even though I'd told Tristan he needed to get laid, apparently so did I because I couldn't stop thinking about his mouth and what he could do with it. My dick had been half hard for the entire trip. So lost in thought, I jolted when my phone rang loud and jarring through the speakers. I glanced at the screen and suppressed a groan.

Mom. I debated letting it go to voicemail. No doubt she either wanted me to do something or talk about the upcoming game.

"You going to get that?" Tristan asked, and because I didn't want him to probe me about avoiding my parents, I hit answer.

"What's up?" I asked just to hear her huff in annoyance at the casual greeting.

"The Jenkins, the couple that wanted to see the house next weekend, just called, and we need you to show the house in about an hour." She jumped straight to the point as usual. "I know it's last minute. But we are supposed to meet with the commercial property manager in half an hour. We are on our way out. Can you do it?"

"Sure. " I glanced at Tristan, who was already eyeing me back with a cocked brow. "I'm on my way now."

"Thanks. We owe you. Let me know how it goes." She hung up, and the call disconnected before I could even reply.

"Will do," I mumbled to myself. My lips were already

moving without my permission. "Change of plans. I have to go show a house. You want to tag along?"

Tristan shrugged. "Fine with me."

I pulled off the highway and made a U-turn to begin the twenty-minute drive to the Greenford property outside Sugar Land with heavy bass thumping through the speakers as the miles passed.

As we pulled off the exit ramp, Tristan turned down the volume. "You have to do this often?"

"Unfortunately." I flicked on my blinker at the stoplight.

"I can't blame your parents. I bet you sell a lot of houses," he stated.

When the light turned green, I turned onto Main Street, heading toward the outskirts of town before taking a quick glance his way. "Why's that?"

"Don't play stupid with me. You know the women, and men probably, want to ride your dick." His tone was so casual, as if he hadn't just insinuated everyone wanted to sleep with me. Did that include him? I'd suspected he was into me, even before Nash had confirmed it, but with his regular reminders that he wasn't, who knew what was going on in that intriguingly weird as hell head of his.

I groaned under my breath. I knew I shouldn't ask, but I couldn't resist messing with Tristan, paying him back for the torture he'd put me through, talking about certain skills he possessed—and I might have wanted to know more than I should. "You saying you want to fuck me?"

Tristan scoffed. "You wish. I don't fit any type of mold, so you can't lump me in with the general population. I don't do jocks."

Sure he didn't. I wasn't blind, and I'd caught Tristan staring at me more times than I could count. Maybe I'd noticed because I'd been eyeing him right back. Again, I had no business thinking about Tristan in that way. Not with the secret still looming between us. I decided it was better not to respond because I didn't trust myself to not say something that would sound like an admission that I was bisexual —yet another secret I'd withheld from my new *best friend*.

The next five minutes were spent in silence. We passed multiple housing developments until we reached areas where moderately-sized homes were built on large plots of open land.

The Greenford house was a white brick ranch-style home centered on five acres of lush land that was carefully maintained by our landscapers. I scanned the yard as we pulled down the driveway, double-checking everything was in top condition. I knew curb appeal alone could either sell a home or turn someone away.

As always, it was immaculate. My parents never settled for less than perfect, which included me—as much as they could manage anyway. It was one of the reasons I loved my beat-up truck as much as I did. It represented rebellion at its finest.

Tristan whistled next to me. "This place looks more fake than an orange spray tan."

"Fake?" I snorted.

"Unreal. Plastic. Like a model of a home, instead of a livable one." He popped open the truck door, and I followed suit, meeting him at the front of the truck. I tried to see the property from his point of view.

Tristan wasn't wrong—at least compared to his own eccentric style. Despite the blue pops of color embedded along with the white azaleas in the flower beds, the place lacked personality of any kind. Something I hadn't realized until Tristan had pointed it out.

Pushing the thought aside, I headed toward the front

door. "I'm sure the people who move in will do something with it. The presentation is half of what sells it. People like a blank slate."

"Whatever you say." Tristan followed behind me as we climbed the short set of steps to the concrete porch, which was surrounded by a wooden railing. The keys were in the lockbox, and I quickly entered the code before entering the house.

The interior was void of furniture but showcased new dark walnut-stained hardwood floors. The scent of freshly painted eggshell-colored walls hovered in the air.

Tristan walked over to the wall of windows in the living room that provided a wide view of the backyard dotted with tall oak trees. While he faced away from me, I scanned his back before landing on the ass he was convinced—and I had to reluctantly agree—was perfectly rounded and filled out his tight black jeans in a way that made me want to...

I shook my head and cleared my throat. "Be right back."

Striding away before I got caught staring, I moved through the house, making sure everything was clean and dust-free before I headed back to where I left Tristan. He was no longer standing by the window, so I searched the house, finding him in the master bedroom. Spinning in a slow circle, he looked underwhelmed at best. I leaned against the door frame watching him. "Not the kind of place you'd live in?"

He shrugged before glancing over at me, wiggling his eyebrows. "I like that it's far from the other houses, so I can be as loud as I want."

"Is sex all you ever think about?" I cocked a brow and just barely managed to keep myself from reaching down to adjust my dick. It didn't mind in the slightest that Tristan's mind was dirtier than all of my teammates combined, which was impressive.

He smirked. "Like you said. I need to get la—"

Pushing away from the door, I lunged for him, my hand shooting out, covering his mouth before he could keep saying shit that made my dick hard. "Seriously—"

A wet swipe across my palm made me freeze. I narrowed my gaze at him. "Did you just lick me?"

He hummed in acknowledgment to my question before gripping my wrist and dragging my hand just far enough away to wrap his pouty lips around my finger. He gave it a powerful suck that fucked with my head so bad that I didn't even pull it away. I let him worship my finger as if he were on his knees with my cock in his mouth. The longer I stood immobile, staring at my finger sliding in and out of the warm wet heat of his mouth, the harder he sucked.

With more self-control than I was aware I possessed, I snapped out of the haze, reminding myself, again, why messing around was a bad idea. The secrets between us were just too much to bear.

Yanking my hand back, Tristan gave a pout I wasn't so sure was fake, and I had to bite my tongue before I forgot all of the reasons we couldn't do this. Didn't matter how much I wanted it. Swallowing hard, I wiped my hand on my jeans. "I can't believe you just did that."

"Yes, you can." He quirked his lips. "What I'm struggling with is why you let me." Shit. I was dangerously close to outing myself, and when he glanced down at the bulge in my pants, I really had no idea what to say. He saved my ass without knowing it. "Don't sweat it, quarterback. I told you my mouth—"

Fuck me. I snapped. All the taunting and sexual comments from the last week roared to the surface of my brain and erupted, no longer under my control. Grabbing Tristan's shoulders, I spun him around. Stalking forward as he stepped back, eyes full of questions, I shoved him against the wall and pinned him there with my body. Hovering over him, I gave him a chance to push me away.

Tristan stared back with those wide eyes before taunting me once again, "I might be a little confused, but don't stop now because you already fucked up. You want to kiss me, so do it."

Every single warning bell only created a low hum compared to the electricity crackling in my veins, making that warning too easy to ignore. A deep growl rumbled in my chest as I slammed my mouth against his, slanting my head and groaning when he parted his perfect lips. *Fuck. I knew it.* His wicked tongue stroked along mine, tangling together... and then he sucked it like he had my finger. *I was gone.* Fuck the consequences. I'd deal with that shit later. The only thing I wanted was *more.* Fuck, I wanted more.

Tristan fucked my mouth in a clash of tongue, teeth, and lips. I gave it to him harder. Deeper. Swallowing his moans, I was fucking drowning in the languid sounds vibrating against my chest. I don't know when I pressed my cock against him, grinding and cursing when he lifted up on his toes to meet me, dry humping me as if he was dying for my cock. Hell, I was dying to give it to him—to shove inside his ass, wrapped in the heat of his tight little body as I filled him over and over. The visual in my mind made my nuts draw tight, but I couldn't stop the impending train wreck if my life depended on it. Zero fucks given if I came in my pants.

Sliding my hands down his sides, I reached around, gripping his ass, lifting him up until he wrapped his legs around my hips so I could feel every bit of his dick against mine. He was hard as hell and clung to the back of my head, sliding his fingers through my hair. I must have lost my cap, but I didn't care. He tugged at the strands, driving me crazier and trapping my lips with his, as if I could possibly tear myself away. My failed restraint was fucking laughable at this point. I soaked in his moans and reveled in his tight little body squirming against mine.

Doesn't fuck jocks, my ass. What would he do if I ripped open his fly and grabbed his cock? Would he drop to his knees and put that talented mouth to work? Would he welcome me if I jerked his pants down so I could finger fuck his ass before I licked his asshole until he was begging me to fuck him? With the way he was kissing me, I was positive we were on the same page. We couldn't seem to get close enough.

Tristan wiggled his slim fingers between our bodies and yanked at the button on my jeans. *Oh, hell yes.*

"I want to touch your dick," he whispered against my lips. "I want you to fuck my hand."

Fucking gladly. I could only groan in response as I made just enough space for him to reach my zipper.

"Hello?" The deep sound of a man's voice was akin to being doused in ice-cold water.

I jerked back, quickly removing Tristan's hand from my fly and lowering him to the ground. Fuck. I adjusted my dick so roughly I winced in pain, fixed my pants and shirt before glancing at Tristan. He was a mess of tangled hair and bruised lips.

"Fuck," I growled out loud this time. Now that the heat fizzled between us, Tristan looked confused. The question in his gaze made me swallow hard. I'd have to face the music later because I was all too aware of the tapping heels coming down the hall.

"Bathroom's in there." I pointed toward a door inside the room. "Can you look a little less..."

"Almost fucked?" he suggested, and I didn't have time to argue, especially because Tristan was right.

I ran my hands through my hair, searching the floor for my hat. I found it carelessly tossed into the center of the room and slid it back on. "Yes. I gotta go deal with these people."

He pushed off the wall. "Fine. But I have questions."

Of course he did and rightfully so. But what the fuck was I supposed to say in response? There was no backpedaling out of what I'd impulsively done. One secret was out, exploding in the space between us. I wanted to fuck Tristan. And I wanted it bad.

I tore my gaze away and took a deep breath. "Just come out when you're done, okay?"

He muttered an agreement, so without glancing back, I left the bedroom, finding the older couple standing in the middle of the kitchen. "Hello, you must be the Jenkins. Sorry about the delay."

I held my hand out and shook the man's hand before reaching toward his wife to do the same.

"Oh, it's fine," she responded with a smile. "Sorry for letting ourselves in. We knocked, and no one responded, but we saw the truck outside."

No one had responded because I'd been busy sticking my tongue down Tristan's throat. I gave an apologetic grin. "No problem at all. Would you like to start in the living room?"

TEN

TRISTAN

NEITHER MEMPHIS nor I said a word as we drove back toward my apartment. I didn't bother hiding the fact that I was staring at him as he visibly brooded, glaring a hole through the windshield. Pinched lips, and brows drawn into a frown, he ran a thick finger over them absently as he gripped the steering wheel so hard I wondered if it would crack.

The awkward silence was unsettling, and we both knew we needed to talk about what had happened in that bedroom. It was fine. I didn't mind starting the conversation. "Thanks for sharing your tongue with me, I think... But why did you—"

"Can we not..." Memphis blew out a shuddered breath. "Can we just not talk about that right now?"

I clamped my lips together, unable to determine how serious he was. Memphis had to know by now that me keeping my mouth shut, not talking about that kiss was going to be pretty much impossible for me. Not knowing what he was thinking was killing me, so I had to push him the only way I knew how—by talking dirty to get him to break the silence. "I mean, you seemed to enjoy it. Actually, you seemed pretty much down to fuck."

"So much for not talking about it," Memphis muttered and then released a heavy sigh. "I'm bisexual, Tristan." He shot a quick glance my way, but I barely reacted. While there was a brief flicker of surprise, it was quickly replaced by confirmation of what I had already worked out when he'd pressed me against the wall. "No one knows, except Nash, so you can't tell anyone."

I waved him off, trying to defuse his nerves about the earth-shattering confession. "Who am I going to tell?" I froze. "Hold up. If Nash knows, then Rendon knows." There was no way Nash had kept that from him. Still, I waited for Memphis to respond.

Finally, he nodded. "Yeah, Rendon would have put it together at that pool party at Bishop's where he and Nash got into it... if it can be called that. I'm the one who found his profile—"

"'That asshole," I cursed, because Rendon had known I'd been into Memphis before I'd decided I wasn't anymore. "I can't believe he kept that from me."

Memphis cocked a brow. "Why were you so interested? You're not into jocks, remember?"

I scowled and lied through my pearly white teeth. "I'm not. You attacked my lips, and they were unprepared for battle."

"What in the actual fuck are you saying most of the time?" Memphis smirked, but it quickly fell away. "It won't happen again."

My whole body tensed. "Why the fuck not? You can't tell me you didn't want it."

"Because I don't fuck around with people I know, and I'm not in the market for a boyfriend." Memphis bit his lip as he went back to staring down the asphalt passing under the truck.

I got a distinct feeling there was more to it, but my pride had just taken a massive beating. "Good. Me too. Wouldn't touch you again if you begged me to. Because I. Don't. Do. Jocks. So next time, keep your stupidly amazing lips to yourself."

Memphis growled. "Tristan, don't be mad. It's not you—"

"I'm not mad." My hand snapped out, and I cranked the volume up, letting the heavy bass fill the cab and vibrate beneath my ass. Was he seriously about to give me the ridiculous *"it's not you, it's me"* line? I crossed my arms over my chest and slouched in my seat. I wasn't sure if I was mad, actually. Maybe it was the disappointment I was feeling. Perhaps it was smart to make sure it didn't happen again. It wasn't like it would go anywhere, and a quick hookup might get awkward when we still hung out. Or maybe if we hooked up, he'd even ditch me all together afterward. Hell, maybe he would ditch me now anyway.

I was relieved when I spotted my apartment complex in the distance and relaxed when he pulled off onto the service road. As soon as he turned into the parking lot, I unlatched my seatbelt, totally prepared for a tuck and roll to escape the awkwardness.

Memphis slowed next to the curb, and I popped my door open, ready to jump out.

"Tristan, wait," Memphis blurted, and I paused, glancing over my shoulder with a raised brow. "I have an away game this weekend, but there's a Halloween party the night after."

Why was he telling me? "And?"

"And you need to pick out a costume," he informed me like he was the boss of me.

My breathing did this weird thing, where it stopped working, causing me to feel a spinning sensation. I snapped out of it, sucking in a deep breath. Maybe I was more worried he'd abandon ship than I'd thought. "Why? I don't remember agreeing to go."

"You're going. This whole...*thing* doesn't change anything. If I have to drag you to that party kicking and screaming, I will." A dimple popped, and it really did seem like Memphis was completely unaffected by what we'd done. But I called bullshit. He'd been into it, and he'd fucking started it.

I studied the cocksure bastard. His eyes locked with mine as if daring me to say no, so of course, I did. "Nope. Jock parties are not my scene."

His smile fell into a frown. "You *are* mad."

"I am *not* mad." I scoffed. I'd had a heart-to-heart with myself and had decided Memphis was right and told him so. "You were right. Shouldn't have happened and never will again."

His lips clamped shut, and his nostrils flared. "Right," he gritted out.

"Uh-huh," I ground out.

He quickly glanced out the front windshield, jaw ticcing. "Pick out a costume, or I will."

When he looked back at me, I could tell he was serious. With a huff, I slid from the truck, hopping down onto the ground. "Fine. But I get to pick yours too."

Memphis looked ready to argue but then surprised me when he just shook his head. "Tris, you better not pick anything stupid."

I grinned. "Stupid to me? Or you?"

Shaking his head, I could tell he already regretted the decision. "Take pictures so I can veto stuff."

Rolling my eyes, I took a step back. I wasn't going to let Memphis take the fun out of being able to witness his reaction to whatever I chose. "Pfft. Okay."

He attempted to frown, but his lips twitched with the effort, resulting in a crooked grin. "You aren't going to send me any pictures, are you?"

I only smiled before shutting the door to the sound of his sigh. Turning my back, I strolled casually to the stairs. I didn't hear his truck pull away, so I knew Memphis had waited until I'd gone inside again. For such a jerk, he was a thoughtful one, at least.

From the time I'd found out Rendon had kept the secret of Memphis being into guys, I'd been stewing on that fact, so after snagging a bottle of water from the refrigerator, I plopped down on the couch and called Rendon, turning on the video as my phone rang.

The screen lit up with the image of my best friend, well, not my best friend anymore since he was a liar. I narrowed my eyes at him and his face broke into a grin.

"Why do you look like you're about to go on a rant?" Rendon pushed his square-framed glasses up the bridge of his nose before swiping his blond hair from his forehead.

"Because I've been cruelly deceived by my ex-best friend. I can't believe you didn't tell me Memphis was into doing guys."

His eyebrows shot high. "I don't know what..." He squinted. "Wait, how do you know about Memphis?"

My back stiffened. "So Nash did tell you."

Rendon hesitated. "Yes, but how did you find out? You're not stalking him, are you?"

"What?" I was insulted. Yes, I was probably a little unpredictable, but stalking? I hadn't sunk that low. "Of course not. Memphis has bullied his royal jockass—that's like jackass for football players, and I really feel like that term needs to be a thing—way into being my new best friend."

Rendon frowned. "I have so many questions. How exactly did that happen? When did that happen? Did he tell you he was bisexual, or are you reaching because you want him to be? Also, jock *whatever* is never going to be a thing. And I thought I was your best friend."

Not anymore. The liar. "I told you he harassed me into it at a party I went to a few weekends ago, and I might have told him off. But only a little bit," I swore. "Then he was all *'we are hanging out, Tristan. We are going to be friends, Tris.'* Yes, he gave me a nickname and everything. He forced me to go do something. And you know what he did? He took me mudding. *Me.* And he didn't tell me he was into banging guys too, exactly." I hedged because I wasn't sure if Memphis would be mad. With Rendon, there was a good chance he would tell Nash everything. "Wait! All of Nash's friends had to pull us out of the mud, and they probably would have told Nash. You're just pretending not to know again, aren't you?"

Rendon's cheeks flushed, and he pushed his square-framed glasses up the bridge of his nose. "I swear I didn't." He glanced to his side. "Did you know?"

He was clearly speaking to his boyfriend, Nash Sterling, one of Memphis's old teammates before he went pro. I should have known he would be right next to Rendon.

"Uh..." The deep voice sounded strained. He'd been caught red-handed keeping a secret from Rendon.

"You did," Rendon accused, voice rising before he glanced back at me. "I really didn't know. But I no longer trust my boyfriend, so can we pick up this conversation later?"

"Oh, come on, babe," Nash muttered. "I knew you'd worry, and you know Tristan isn't going to listen to a damn thing you say."

"Hey!" I damn near shouted. Who was Nash to point out my inability to make good decisions?

"It's true." Rendon cocked a brow. "But he's still in trouble. I'll call you tomorrow on my lunch break."

"Fine." I sighed and shut down the call.

Once the quiet of the apartment was all that surrounded me, my thoughts immediately swung back to the kiss. Memphis hadn't just kissed me. He'd attempted to suck my soul from my body. It was never going to happen again. But before I wiped my memory clean, I was going to let the fantasy play out one time, as if that couple had never shown up. I leaned back into the cushions and unzipped my jeans, humming when I finally wrapped my hand around my dick.

Just the one time, I lied to myself.

THE WEEKEND SUCKED. It was only Saturday night, but I hadn't been able to talk to Memphis much because his coach had run the team ragged, getting them ready for the game he'd played today. I'd watched the whole thing, proud of myself as I paid attention to the entire game—well, at least when the offense was on the field. I mean, I was a shit friend if I missed one of Memphis's games, right? It was my job to watch his muscular thighs and tight ass as he ran around, toned arms pumping the ball before letting it fly. Yep, I was the best friend ever because I'd never taken my eyes off him.

The Saints had won, but only barely with a last-minute

score. Thank fuck, because after the last real convo Memphis and I'd had the day he kissed me, I really didn't want to deal with a brooding quarterback, because it made my dick hard. That wasn't part of the whole forget-the-kiss pact.

I was surprised when my phone rang, flashing Memphis's name, as I lay in bed—more so when I noticed it was a video call. *Shit.* I hadn't gone anywhere today, so my face was devoid of any makeup. Whatever. I hit answer and held back a groan when a freshly showered quarterback showed up on my screen, hair still wet as a drop rolled down his sharp cheekbone.

Annoyed because he was making it impossible to not think about his mouth on mine, I sighed. "How may I help you? Shouldn't you be out celebrating?"

His brows shot high. "You watched the game?"

I scowled. "No, I watched TV, but you were on there, taking up the whole screen."

Memphis grinned, dimples popping with the boyish smile. "And your remote was broken?"

"As a matter of fact, it is," I lied, and Memphis snorted. Dick. "I'll have to look into ordering a new one."

"Probably a good idea," he agreed, still smug. "What are you doing?"

"Lying in bed." *Not thinking about you,* I tacked on in my head because one could also lie to oneself. "Don't look at my face."

Memphis snorted. "What exactly am I supposed to look at then?"

"Anything else?" I suggested. "I didn't expect you to call."

"I've already seen you without makeup when I picked

you up that first morning." He squinted. "You look different. Younger."

I waved my hand around my face. "Sparkly clean. You can count yourself among the few that have witnessed my makeup-free baby face."

"You don't look like a baby. You look—" Memphis cleared his throat. "I like it." I only had half a second to process that Memphis *liked it* before he changed the topic. "I'll be home tomorrow morning sometime. Probably closer to noon. Did you pick out costumes?"

The Halloween party was tomorrow night, and I wasn't sure that Memphis wouldn't be too tired to go after the long trip. Not to mention it would be a night before classes—not ideal, but with the Saints being away, the whole campus would suffer the next morning just so they could attend. "I did. You're going to love them."

He groaned. "Something tells me that's not the case."

I shrugged. "Ye of little faith."

"When it comes to your randomness? I'm not going to argue, plus I'm pretty sure you'd enjoy torturing me."

"After the mud incident, I'd say I have the right to do that." Tit for tat.

Memphis smirked. "I'm getting you back in the mud eventually."

"Like hell." I was firmly standing my ground—dry ground—on that one.

His smile was slow right before he yawned. "What did you do this weekend?"

"All kinds of things. I went to the beach, flew in a helicopter, and partied with some gay porn stars." I battled a smile when his grin widened.

"You never left your bed, did you?"

I huffed. "I ordered takeout, napped a lot, and dragged

my ass to the shower once. Oh, and I finished an assign-ment. But I actually did watch some porn, and there was definitely a party. Like a gang bang at a birthday party. It was hot."

Memphis chuckled. "Oversharing is always going to be a thing with you, isn't it?"

"Probably. But it's too late to bail now. You are stuck with me."

Memphis shrugged, and the camera jostled as he lay back into what appeared to be lush white cotton sheets. "I can handle that."

"Are you sharing a room?" I blurted, not liking the idea of it at all.

He shook his head. "Was supposed to be sharing with Logan, but I'm pretty sure his boyfriend tagged along, and Logan snuck down to his room. Doubt I'll see him until he sneaks back in before we leave."

I knew who Logan was, though I'd never really spoken to him. Boyfriend or not, I was glad Memphis was alone. Of course, I wouldn't tell him that. "Lucky you."

He hummed in agreement. "What was your assignment?"

I groaned as I adjusted myself on the bed, propping myself up further on the pillows stacked behind me. "Boring history essay."

"Not into history?" Memphis asked as he let out another yawn.

I'd watched him exhaust himself on the field and knew he had to be battling sleep, so why he was pressing to keep me on the phone, I didn't know. "I prefer to look toward the future. Nothing good lives in the past."

A thoughtful look crossed his face before Memphis glanced away. His Adam's apple bobbed before he looked back at the camera. "So, what's the goal when you graduate?"

I had a few years to think about that or come to a final decision. What I wanted to do didn't pay a lot, but the reward could be so much greater. Memphis might probe if I told him the truth about wanting to be a counselor for gay kids who might have found themselves in similar situations to what I'd experienced. I was resilient, or at least I liked to think so. But there would always be guys out there that had it worse than what I'd gone through, couldn't handle it, and weren't ready to come out, needing someone to confide in anonymously.

Without much pause, I quipped, "Professional mourner."

Memphis choked on a laugh. "Really?"

Rolling my eyes, I shook my head. "So gullible. Obviously, I want to be a rancher and own more cows than sticks of eyeliner I have loaded into my top drawer next to my butt plugs."

"Liar," Memphis drawled as drowsiness lowered his lids. He must have been barely awake to let the comment go so easily without reprimand.

"I could if I wanted to." How hard could it be? "But you're right. A coroner is much more my speed."

He blinked at me, and I did my best to hold back the chuckle, staring at him blank-faced. "You serious?"

I nodded emphatically. "Yep."

"I don't believe you." He squinted, attempting to call my bluff.

"Think what you want." I lifted a shoulder.

"I think you're never going to tell me." His grin was lazy.

"Fine, since you keep pressuring me. An outdoor tour guide, of course."

His dimples deepened. "I know you're lying about that one, Tristan; I've seen you outdoors."

Eh, I couldn't argue with that one.

When I remained quiet because I didn't trust myself not to blurt out the truth, Memphis rubbed his tired reddening eyes. "Fine, I can take a hint. Will you at least tell me what you are majoring in since you won't tell me what you plan on doing with that insane brain of yours?"

I could do that. Even though it would likely lead to questions, that didn't mean I had to answer them. And I found myself wanting to tell him the truth. He reminded me so much of that guy who kissed me that night back on the worst evening of my life. Even though I'd firmly separated the two in my head, Memphis seemed genuine in the way he wanted to know more about me. "You're relentless. I'm working on a psychology degree."

Memphis raised his brows. I was sure that wasn't the answer he'd expected at all.

"Trust me. I know it's stupid. My people skills?" I snorted.

Memphis's features relaxed. "You want to work with people? Like help them or dissect them?"

"I'm not going to turn into a serial killer, hacking people to bits." I snorted.

"That's not what I meant, and you know it." He stared at me so hard, it felt like he was piercing my soul. I couldn't help it. The truth came tumbling out.

"I want to help them—or at least try to. I... I had something shitty happen to me in high school." I took a deep breath. "I could have used someone to talk to. There was this guy the night it happened. I didn't know him... Hell, I couldn't even see his face. He was the reason I was able to push through the experience, embrace who I am. Instead of the incident tearing me apart, I grew confident and... Well, you see who I am today. If I could open an online clinic where guys could meet with me anonymously... I want to pay it forward. Help someone else who is struggling. Does that make sense?"

Memphis grew quiet, and his expression unreadable.

"My school counselor would have clutched her knockoff pearls if I'd tried to go to her about it," I continued, not wanting to reveal what exactly had happened. I didn't want Memphis to know what I'd done. How weak I'd been at one point, giving in to a guy that was such an asshole.

Memphis swallowed so hard it came across the phone as if he was right next to me. "I think you'd be an amazing counselor."

My lips twisted, unconvinced he was right. It was the main reason I hadn't made a final decision. "I don't know. I'm sort of a mess myself most of the time."

The admission surprised me, mostly because I hadn't realized how true it was until that moment. Memphis appeared unfazed, though.

He gave a slight shake of his head. "Who isn't?"

"Yeah." Nodding, I sighed. "Well, I guess I have a few years to get my shit together at least."

"You do," he agreed before pausing. "I haven't told anyone this, but my parents put an ungodly amount of pressure on me every day about going pro. I've thought about quitting more times than I can count, but I can't. I love the game and want to play for as long as my body allows. But they make it a struggle, and I wish they'd stop and just let me enjoy it."

He'd never told anyone? Why now, and why me? "Have you told them how you feel and asked them to back off?"

Memphis grimaced. "Not really. I should have, and I

plan to. They've just supported me my whole life. My dad played in college and was a sure thing for the NFL before he was injured. He loved the game as much as I do. I guess I feel a little guilty if I ask him to leave me alone about it when he had his dreams taken away. I don't have any siblings, so I guess he lives vicariously through me where football is concerned."

I considered his words. "I get it, I think. I'm an only child too, so my parents worry about me to the extreme. There's no brothers or sisters to distract them." I moved on because he appeared ready to question me further about what had happened. "But maybe you should tell them how you feel. They might even understand because your dad experienced the pressure the league offers all on its own."

I may not have been a huge football fan, but even I knew how rigorous the players' schedules were. The heavy expectations rested on their shoulders to represent the school. Some had scholarships depending on their performance on the field.

Memphis yawned again as his eyes drooped further. "Maybe."

He was barely conscious at this point, so I said, "You need to sleep."

Memphis didn't answer. A slight snore whispered through his lips before the phone must have fallen from his grip, granting me a bland view of the hotel room ceiling. For some reason, I couldn't hang up. Maybe Rendon had a right to be concerned. Was it considered stalking or creepy to just listen to someone sleep? Probably. Leaving the phone on my pillow, I closed my eyes, falling asleep to the sound of Memphis breathing.

ELEVEN
MEMPHIS

MY SIMPLE, rustic home sat deep in the woods in the unpopulated outskirts of Sugar Land. A gravel drive led to my log cabin with both a front and back porch that stretched the entire length of the house. The grove of trees that grew tall all around the property provided shade from the Texas heat and homes to birds, squirrels, and other wildlife. An open floor plan of the den, kitchen, and dining room—all of which would have fit in my parents' living room—made up one room with exposed beams across the ceiling. I preferred the simplicity of the unadorned blond oak cabinets and countertops that made up a single wall, and the small wooden dining table with only two chairs. Two beige cloth recliners faced an old stone fireplace, leaving a lot of empty space, but I didn't need much. Even the undersized appliances were dated, discolored with years of use and probably needed to be replaced.

The sun broke through the dense trees that swayed gently in the breeze, leaving flickering shadows dancing on the tabletop where I sat staring out the open window. I absently picked at my vegetable and cheese omelet while I obsessed over the conversation with Tristan from last night.

My stomach was tied in knots as I forced down each bite of my late morning breakfast. The same thoughts had raced through my mind the entire bus ride home from the hotel. As the miles passed by, I had felt Logan side-eyeing me from where he'd sat in the seat beside mine, but I hadn't been able to bring myself to engage in the banter that had flowed between my teammates. I hadn't been able to fake my way through the guilt weighing heavily on my shoulders.

I should have told Tristan the truth before things had progressed to sharing personal truths with each other. I *needed* to explain to him why I'd kept my distance for so long, more so now than ever. I hadn't been prepared at all for how serious the conversation had turned. One minute I had my normal smart-mouthed Tristan. The next, without being aware of it, he was telling me I'd changed his life in the most unexpected way. I had no idea I'd impacted him that much, and now I felt like shit for keeping the truth from him.

My fork clattered onto the plate as I scrubbed a hand over my face, feeling the prickles of my unshaven jaw beneath my palm. Fuck. How could I tell him now? After his admission, I wasn't even sure how to start that conversation. In all likelihood, he would feel betrayed by the one person he'd apparently been so grateful to have by his side that night.

He is the reason I was able to push through the experience, embrace who I am. Instead of the incident tearing me apart, I grew confident.

I blinked hard as I replayed his words and slouched

back in my chair, groaning in frustration. There were so many things he didn't know.

Tristan wasn't aware that the kiss at the rental property hadn't been our first. He had no idea I was the guy who sat next to him beneath that tree, who had stolen his first kiss. And the picture he'd sent me of his dick? There was no way Tristan could possibly know that had been me he'd messaged. The lies by omission and secrets were eating away at my conscience.

This whole situation had disaster written all over it. My thoughts were a foggy tangle of doubt and unease over the consequences that would follow my overdue confession. One thing pierced through the doubt, clear and bright—a fact I couldn't deny. I wanted Tristan. Even though I'd told him we'd pretend the kiss that almost went too far never happened, I couldn't forget the way he'd felt and tasted on my tongue. The way neither of us had held back with him pressed against the wall, my body pinning him there. I'd given in to the craving I'd tried my best to ignore, unprepared for the explosion of desperate need that had ignited between us. I had to get closer to him. To take what I wanted and claim what belonged to me—except Tristan didn't and couldn't belong to me. I'd have to keep my hands —and other anatomy—to myself.

I should have ended things, but I was selfish and wasn't ready to walk away. But Tristan? He'd more than likely do that on his own once he learned the truth.

Between the lack of sleep, the long trip home, and the overwhelming guilt over the betrayal I'd committed, I was exhausted. I wasn't equipped to handle the situation at the moment, so I stood and carried my uneaten food to the trash. After rinsing my plate and sticking it in the dishwasher, I heaved myself down the hall, collapsed on my oversized bed, and was asleep before my head hit the pillow.

I must have dozed most of the day because when my phone chimed, jolting me awake, my room had darkened with the setting sun. Rubbing the sleep from my eyes, I grabbed my phone, spotting the text from Tristan, and checked the time. It was already eight thirty-two. *Shit.*

I swiped over to the text.

Tristan: *You are two minutes late.*

Still groggy, I quickly tapped out a response as I rolled out of bed on stiff legs and stretched my back.

Me: *Sorry. I was out cold. Give me twenty.*

Without waiting for a response, I took the quickest shower of my life before slipping on a pair of jeans and a forest green t-shirt. I snatched my wallet and keys, checking my phone again.

Tristan: *You better hurry. I can't wait to see you in this costume. And I look cute as hell.*

A rough laugh rumbled in my chest, erasing all thoughts of the problems I'd been obsessing over. I was almost positive I'd refuse to wear whatever insane outfit he'd bought.

Me: *Leaving now.*

Picking up Tristan was becoming routine, although unnecessary considering he owned a car. But it just made sense for me to swing by since we always seemed to be going to the same place. Together. Something I would never have considered a possibility a few weeks ago.

I turned into the now-familiar apartment complex within ten minutes, my headlights lighting up the red brick. I pulled into a space close to the stairs that led to his unit and hopped out.

Taking the stairs two at a time, I reasoned with myself that I was in such a hurry so I wouldn't have to listen to

Tristan rant more than I'd already prepared for. Not because I *needed* to see him.

Before I could knock on his door, it swung open, revealing his tight little body dressed as a police officer, oddly paired with a devil-horned headband. I burst out laughing. "What the fuck are you wearing?"

Tristan rolled his eyes. "Bad cop, obviously. Which makes you"—he brandished a fucking halo from behind his back and held it out to me—"good cop. Of course, you have to put on the uniform first."

He opened the door wider and turned on his heels. I scowled at his back for two reasons. One, I had no intention of wearing the stupid halo. Two, the outfit he wore was super tight, hugging his ass in a way I really didn't want other people to see. *It was mine.* Except it wasn't. My nostrils flared as I reminded myself I hadn't spent the entire day thinking over the situation just to fuck it up the moment I laid eyes on him again. Instead, I focused on the one part I could control. "I'm not wearing that."

Tristan pulled a bag from the coat hook mounted on the wall and paused, jutting out his bottom lip as he scanned me over. "You're right, Officer Hale. I've been a bad boy. *You* should definitely be the one to go as the bad cop. I have the handcuffs and everything so you can punish me properly."

"*Tristan,*" I growled. Not gonna lie. My cock didn't mind the idea of punishing him, spanking his round ass. "Get in the truck," I ground out before I could put a mental image to that dirty thought.

"Seriously? You're not going to wear any of it?" He frowned, and I bit back a suffering sigh.

Holding out my hand, I tried not to let the pleased smile that crossed his face affect me. But then I pulled out the outfit and bit my lip to keep from refusing, yet again. He'd been serious. The costume was the exact same as his, except much larger.

"At least try it on." Tristan circled around me and attempted to shove me forward in the direction of the bathroom. "You're like an unmovable rock. Like one of those prehistoric ones that are practically glued to the tectonic plate itself," he huffed, pushing harder when he still hadn't managed to move me. "Except, even those shift around more than you do," he grunted.

I snorted a laugh. "Fine. But I can't promise I'm wearing it."

"Lame." Tristan finally stopped pushing me when I headed toward the bathroom of my own free will.

After shutting the door, I stared at the police uniform before laying it out on the counter. I hadn't dressed up for Halloween in almost a decade. Even when I was younger, I went as a zombie football player every year. I tugged off my clothes and slipped into the costume, examining myself in the mirror. I guess it wasn't *that* bad. He could have chosen something much worse, and it wouldn't have shocked me at all.

A swift knock rattled the door.

"Let me see," Tristan's muffled voice demanded. I opened the door and watched as Tristan's eyes widened and his mouth dropped open. His gaze filled with heat as it traveled over my body before jerking back up to meet my eyes. "You're right. You shouldn't wear a costume. Back in your clothes you go," he encouraged with a head shake to persuade me to follow his instructions.

He attempted to close the door, but I stuck out my foot, keeping it open. "Why? You were so determined to get me in this thing, and now I kind of like it."

Tristan huffed, and an annoyed frown tilted his lips. "Yeah, and other people will too."

My lips twitched. "Why is that a bad thing again?"

He scowled, brows furrowing before he turned and stomped off, shouting in no particular direction, "It's a *great* idea. Totally awesome, really. I don't even care. Everyone is going to want you to handcuff them and do dirty things to them." Tristan was now in a mood, and I couldn't help but smile as I quickly shoved my clothes in the bag and followed him. He continued ranting, mumbling not so quietly, "Good cop, my ass. He looks like sin and all things kinky and horny."

A puff of breath escaped my lips, no matter how hard I tried to hold in the laugh. "If I didn't know any better, I'd think you had a problem with that."

He spun around, glaring, and pointed a finger at himself. "I don't"—then aiming that same finger at me, he continued—"That's why I said *you* should wear it."

"Right." No reason to point out that he had given a hard *no* before that. Besides, it was a dangerous road to take, asking him to admit he didn't want anyone else to want me. "Well, in that case, I think I'll keep it on."

"Of course you will," Tristan muttered as he gathered his keys and phone.

Biting my lip to keep my mouth shut, I simply asked, "Ready to go?"

"Uh-huh." He was sulking, lips turned down at the sides and avoiding my eyes. I had the urge to kiss that frown from his face.

Thankfully, my train of thought was interrupted when he walked around me and marched out the front door. He barely paused to lock the door behind us before he charged down the steps as I followed behind.

After we climbed in the truck, Tristan remained quiet for the first five minutes of the drive toward the Sigma Chi frat house. I was just beginning to wonder if his bad mood would last all night when I sensed Tristan scooting closer.

I glanced at him, scrutinizing the mischievous grin on his face. "What are you doing?"

"Attempting to put the halo on you without you noticing. Hold still," Tristan ordered while nibbling his lip as he made another attempt to place the stupid thing on my head.

"Not happening." Placing my palm on his side, I easily slid him back to his seat.

He sighed dramatically. "Ninety-nine cents down the drain. Rendon would have totally worn it."

"I doubt that." I laughed quietly, grateful he seemed to have forgotten he was irritated five seconds ago. Tristan looked adorably ridiculous with the horns still on his head, but I doubted he'd appreciate me telling him so. I had no idea why I found it endearing anyway.

He behaved the rest of the drive, which impressed me even though less than ten miles remained.

As we pulled into frat row, it was obvious the party was in full swing. Cars took up almost every available space along the road in both directions. With my stereo off and windows down, the sound of the thumping music coming from Sigma Chi filled the night, begging for a complaint to be filed with the police. No complaints would ever be filed here in Sugar Land because football was religion. Honestly, we pretty much got away with anything and everything we wanted.

Spotting Logan's shiny new ride, I pulled along the curb into the empty spot behind his expensive SUV and glanced at Tristan. "Ready?"

"I guess. You're totally ruining our look, though." He

tossed the halo onto the floor before sliding out of the truck. I really did need to install running boards or something for him. *Or not.* I shook my head over the asinine thought. I wasn't customizing my truck for Tristan because that was beyond crazy.

I watched as he circled around the hood of the truck, his lithe movements in the uniform costume making my dick thicken. The uniform really wasn't forgiving enough to cover up a hard cock, so I jerked my gaze away and stepped down from the truck.

The scent of cigarettes, pizza, and a mixture of colognes and perfumes carried on the light breeze as we crossed the street, winding through the crowd that scattered across both the lawn and porch. A variety of costumes ranging from basic football jerseys and skimpy cheerleaders to vampires and... Was that a full gorilla suit?

This frat house was pretty much the go-to for parties, and I'd seen Tristan here many times, including the night I'd finally spoken to him. Or rather when he'd confronted me. I tipped my chin toward some of my teammates.

"Beer?" I asked Tristan, glancing down at him as we climbed the steps.

He shook his head. "Not much of a drinker."

I wondered if that had to do with what happened to him in high school, but I couldn't ask without coming clean about everything. I'd tell him soon, I promised myself. I had to. Deciding to leave it for another night, I only wanted to have fun tonight. Because if he did ditch me, which I wouldn't blame him for, I at least needed this. Even if I didn't deserve it. "I'll grab us some water then."

As soon as we stepped inside, I spotted Logan. He was already headed in our direction through the dimly lit room full of college students, dancing, laughing, and talking a steady hum that broke through the loud music in random bursts. He reached out with a fist, bumping mine before his gaze jerked to Tristan and back to me, brow furrowing. "Sooo...nice costumes," Logan commented.

"Thank you," Tristan replied and beamed a smile at me, clearly happy with the compliment. "Memphis wouldn't wear the halo, so he kinda ruined the effect."

Logan smirked at me. "The halo, huh?"

"Not my idea. That was all Tristan," I defended myself.

Logan's dark brown eyes twinkled with humor. I sighed, knowing I'd probably catch shit for dressing up, especially when I saw he was only wearing his football jersey, as were most of my teammates I noticed when I quickly scanned the packed room.

"Too bad. I really wish you'd have worn it." Logan's lips twitched when I narrowed my eyes.

"Me too." Tristan nodded emphatically in agreement.

Logan grinned wide, flashing pearly white teeth at Tristan before switching his gaze to me. "Hey, can I talk to you for just a second?"

Tristan stepped around me. "I'll go grab those waters."

Logan tipped his chin, and I forced myself not to glance back to check on Tristan. I wasn't sure I'd ever feel completely at ease with him at a party without me by his side after everything he'd brought up again about that night. Stuffing my hands in my pockets, I tilted my head. "What's up?"

"You do realize you two came dressed as a couple, right?" He cocked a brow, and for the first time, I realized what Tristan and I must look like to everyone else. *Shit.*

I shook my head. "Nah, we're just friends."

"Obviously, since you're into girls." His brow dipped. "Unless you aren't."

"The fuck?" My stomach clenched. I'd never had someone ask me the question outright and hadn't been prepared for it. "You know I am. One costume, and all of a sudden I'm gay?"

Logan raised his hands, moving out of the way of a drunk guy stumbling through the door. "Just fucking with you, man. Sort of anyway. We're in the way. Come on."

He took several steps, but I stayed rooted in place. Logan looked back with a frown. "Problem?"

I glanced toward the kitchen where Tristan had gone. "I want to make sure he can find me."

"You two going to stay glued to each other's side all night?" Logan appeared confused, and I honestly couldn't blame him. I guess we did look like a couple.

Even if I wanted to shake Tristan, which I didn't, I knew he wouldn't let me. He'd hunt me down somehow. I explained, "We came together. I just don't want him to think I ditched him."

For several reasons, I had to make sure he could see me. I didn't like the idea of him feeling abandoned, and less importantly was the thought of him logging onto that stupid app because he was pissed at me. Not happening.

Logan smirked, and I scowled, reading the comment forming on his lips. I repeated, "We're just friends."

Logan burst out laughing, patting me on the shoulder. "Right then. Friends."

"What's that supposed to mean?" I frowned. "Never mind. What did you want to talk about?" I asked to change the subject.

He nodded as if remembering his purpose hadn't been to harass me about Tristan. "Colton and I have been talking about getting out of our condo..."

"And you're looking for a place?" I asked. It made sense

why he'd come to me. His spoiled ass would be looking for a house that most real estate agents wouldn't have access to. When he took a sip of his beer, he nodded before running his thumb over his lips.

"Yeah, Colton wants a dog for some reason." He scowled as if the idea was terrible. "The property doesn't allow pets."

He was so obsessed with his boyfriend it didn't surprise me at all that he'd pack up all his shit and move just to give the guy a dog. "I'll see what I have and send you a list of nearby properties."

Logan nodded. "I'd seriously appreciate that. Speaking of Colton, I need to get going. I was just stopping by, but he should be off work soon, and I need to pick him up."

I knew Colton didn't need to work, not with the cash stacked in Logan's bank account. But I understood all too well Colton's need to make it on his own. "Later, man. I'll send the listings tomorrow."

With a final pat on my shoulder, he headed for the front door. I sensed Tristan before I actually saw him. The faint scent of cinnamon reached me just before his voice.

"Officer Hale," he whistled, handing me a water bottle. "You should see your ass in that thing."

"*Tristan...*" I said sternly, glancing around to make sure no one overheard.

"Yes, sir? Hmm... Never knew I had a thing for authority figures." He shrugged casually.

It appeared forgetting the kiss didn't mean the same thing as stopping the ogling and making inappropriate remarks. Not sure why I was even surprised or how I thought at some point my body wouldn't react to Tristan's words. My dick definitely took notice, and I quickly took his arm, ushering him toward the back door before the outline of my semi was noticed by anyone. "Keep your voice down," I hissed in his ear.

"That *was* me keeping my voice down," Tristan insisted, and he wasn't wrong. Still, he kept quiet for a minute until we stepped out onto the back porch where, thank fuck, only a few people were loitering out on the lawn. Tristan leaned back against the wall, and I moved to the railing, facing him. "Do you think you'll ever come out?" he asked.

Paranoid, I glanced around, again thankful no one was close enough to overhear. "Probably. But football complicates things."

"How?" He cocked his head, confusion in his gaze.

I shook my head. "Even though more and more athletes are coming out, it's still not widely accepted."

"What about Shaw, Bishop, Rush, Torin, and Nash?" he pointed out.

The way things had played out for my friends was something I'd already considered, and that's why I'd said *probably* despite my reservations.

"Rush and Nash were never in the closet. The others didn't go pro. I think my situation is different because people won't be expecting it from me, I guess. I've never given anyone a reason to think I was anything but straight." I sighed. "I hate it, and it sucks, but truthfully, I'm torn."

Tristan hesitated. "Well, I didn't exactly get a choice back home when I was outed in high school."

I stiffened and then cleared my throat, already knowing what happened and not ready for him to bring it back up. My voice was rough when I asked, "No?"

He scowled. "Nope." The *p* popped on his lips. "That was handled for me by an asshole."

I shifted uncomfortably, knowing I should fess up. This felt wrong. "What happened?"

"Doesn't matter. It sucked at the time. Hurt even..." He went silent for a moment before shaking his head. "I just decided to give everyone the middle finger. Because of that guy I told you about."

I nodded, feeling both relieved I'd helped him in some way and angry all over again because of what he'd been put through. "Was it easy? This guy helped you that much?"

"I'm not sure I would have called it easy, but I learned to ignore it. *Them,*" he continued.

"And how did people react when they heard about it?" I asked curiously. After that night, I had wondered what had happened, especially after I'd called the school to report the video. But I'd forced myself not to follow up.

"The situation was handled. I'm not sure how that guy did it, but he... made things easier at school. I think a lot of people were scared they'd get kicked out of school, like the asshole that had..."

"Had what?" I probed because if I hadn't already known, it would have been the natural response. My stomach twisted. As far as how I'd managed to get the guy expelled, football was life in Texas. Anyone paying attention to sports would know who I was. The honest truth was, just like football, my word was religion as far as the administrative staff was concerned. Cocky, yes. True, also yes.

Tristan shook his head as a sigh slipped from his lips. "Never mind."

There it was. Time to either come clean or be an absolute asshole. My heart was thumping so hard in my chest that I wouldn't be shocked if Tristan could hear the erratic beat. I slouched against the rail, staring down at the patio.

Do it, Memphis. Tell him it was you. I tried to convince myself. Earlier tonight, I decided I would do it...just not tonight. But the secret churned in my stomach, and I couldn't handle the pressure and the anxiety of it any longer. "I lied to you," I blurted in a whisper, pinching my eyes closed before peeking at him once again.

Tristan stilled, squaring his shoulders as he pinned me with a curious stare. "About what?"

I cleared my throat but couldn't bring myself to look at him, gaze dipping to the concrete at my feet. "I tried to come out once. A few years ago."

Tristan kicked away from the wall, crossing the porch. The heat from his body warmed my side as he inched closer until his shoulder pressed against my side. "What happened?"

I'd come this far. I had to tell him, so I braced myself for Tristan to walk away. After avoiding him for so long and then hanging out and growing closer over the last few weeks, I was sure I wouldn't handle it well, but Tristan deserved the truth. I took a deep breath, and the story came tumbling out. "One weekend, I went to visit my boyfriend. We'd had a long-distance relationship, but I was ready to come out since I was moving closer to transfer to Sugar Land. I wanted to go public with our relationship—which I soon realized didn't mean quite as much to me as I thought it did. He wasn't on board with the public thing, so we split up. I was still considering coming out, but when I left his house, a guy was sitting on the ground beneath a tree. His black hair hid his face until he looked up at me with ice blue eyes."

Tristan sucked in a hard breath as he went rigid. "No," he whispered. When I glanced at him, he was adamantly shaking his head in disbelief. "No!" he repeated louder.

"He was upset," I choked out, powering through, voice strained. "Some shithead baseball player—"

"What in the actually holy fucking fuck, Memphis?"

Tristan exploded and spun around, backing away so fast his back collided with the side of the house. "You lied to me? You fucking *lied* to me? That's not just lying, Memphis. You kept a huge secret from me. Oh my god, I'm going to pass out." His chest was heaving as he crouched, holding his head in his hands.

I took a step toward him. "Tristan—"

His hand shot up, warning me to stop as his gaze shifted, glaring up at me. "Don't you *Tristan* me, Memphis Hale. I'm so pissed right now. I should have known. I knew those stupid dimples. And oh my God, you kissed me, you dick."

I didn't give a shit if anyone heard at this point. Tristan had every right to do whatever he wanted. His frosty eyes filled with hurt that pierced my chest. "I'm sorry. I didn't know what to do. You said it was easier telling someone you didn't know. There was no way I could have known you would come to Sugar Land. I didn't expect to see you ever again, much less on this campus."

"That's why you ignored me," he said, piecing it together, still glaring.

I nodded, shoving my hands in my pockets.

Tristan shook his head, rolling it side to side as he scoffed in disbelief. "I can't believe this shit. I literally..." His eyes squeezed closed. "Is there anything else you've lied to me about?"

Shit. *Fuck.* I blew out a shaky breath. "Yes."

"Are you serious?" He all but shouted, and I winced. "Well, don't leave me hanging. What else have you conveniently kept to yourself?"

A rough breath thrummed in my chest as I glanced at his pocket, where his phone was outlined through his uniform. "The hookup app." I cleared my throat. "The day of the party when you confronted me, I had seen you at the sandwich shop earlier." I paused. "I'm—"

"You're *Up4it*," he spat, before a humorless laugh whispered through his lips. "I fucking knew it. I can't believe I sent you a picture of my dick, and you didn't feel the need to tell me."

Now was not the time to picture his pierced dick, so I forced the mental image away. "I didn't ask for that picture. I thought it might be you, was pretty sure of it actually. But I wanted to find out for sure and it didn't cross my mind at first that you wouldn't send a head shot."

Tristan snorted. "I did send a head shot."

I bit back a groan. "Not what I meant and you know it." I closed my eyes, because I had to tell him everything. "I saved it."

He went quiet, scary for Tristan. "And jerked off to it?"

Did I really need to respond to that? "Tristan, I'm sorry. If you walk away, I get it. I don't want you to, but I'd understand."

"Walk away? Oh, I'm marching the fuck away. In a parade with 'Fuck you, Memphis' banners and a giant dick float dedicated to a lying, secret-keeping, kiss stealing, jock bastard." He snorted, but there wasn't an ounce of humor behind the sound. "Obviously, that's *you*, unless it applies to others. They can be included in that parade as well."

I rubbed my eyes as I collapsed next to him, sinking against the wall. "You hate me."

It wasn't a question. I made myself look at Tristan so he could have another chance to lay into me again if he needed to. He deserved to show me how much I hurt him. I had to face his wrath.

His nostrils flared as he glanced at me. "I hate you so much."

"What was I supposed to do, Tristan?" I argued. "You think it was easy for me to ignore you when I knew what had happened? Do you think I haven't thought about telling you or how to tell you? I knew when I asked you to go mudding with me, it was a bad idea, knowing I wouldn't be able to tell you the truth, but I still couldn't stand the thought of you thinking that I was the horrible person you'd built up in your mind." I sighed. "I asked myself a hundred times, questioning my every move since the first day I saw you on campus. So you tell me, Tristan. What should I have done?"

"Doesn't matter now, does it?" Tristan pushed to his feet, and I followed. "I'll find my own ride home."

As he went to pass me, I grabbed his arm. "Let me take you home. Please."

"No." He shook off my hand and stepped close, poking his finger to my chest. "I hate you, Memphis Hale. I wish I'd never met you. I wish I'd never set eyes on your stupid dimples. I wish I didn't know you had a birthmark in the shape of Washington. And more so, I wish I had more self-control."

My brows furrowed. "What do—"

Tristan wrapped his hand around the back of my neck, jerking me down and crashing his lips against mine. I froze for less than a second before a deep groan crawled up my throat.

I took his lips, and he parted them, moaning into my mouth. I kissed him as every ounce of need poured out of me, even though I'd sworn to both of us this would never happen again.

He jerked back. Staring at me with narrowed eyes, he repeated, "I hate you."

I swallowed hard, hating those words but knowing I'd

earned them. "That's okay. If you need to hate me, I'll be that for you and..."

"Oh my god. Shut up." He kissed me greedily, his tongue twining with mine while making these little sounds that drove me crazy, needing more of them.

My dick was rock hard as he ground against me, urging me to move with him, letting him feel every solid inch. I kissed him back, craving and wanting more. Needing to feel the friction and swell of his cock against mine, I grabbed his ass and lifted him, swallowing his moan as we dry fucked each other where anyone could see if they cared to look. I wanted him naked, bare dick in my hand. I didn't give two fucks who was around us in that moment, completely wrapped up in the taste of his mouth and the feel of his body writhing against mine. Fuck what anyone thought. Pulling away just enough for our lips to part, I murmured, "Tristan," while panting into his mouth.

"I said zip it, Officer Hale," he snapped before attacking my mouth again.

I didn't need to be told twice. Instead, I kissed him, apologizing, worshipping, and drowning in everything Tristan. Our past, present, and maybe even future.

MEMPHIS TASTED like the worst kind of temptation. A drug you'd never get enough of. The high you would be chasing for the rest of your life if you caved to the bone-deep craving.

I'd caved. Hell, I'd done more than that. I'd started it. And Memphis? He seemed in no hurry to end the weave of tongues, teeth, and lips. He kissed me as if he needed it to breathe.

I was angry. I was grateful. I was fucking confused. Memphis had lied to me. He'd kept two huge secrets from me. I shouldn't be kissing him, but all I wanted was more of the tight grip he had on my ass and the flex of his strong fingers as they kneaded and massaged my flesh through the fabric of the faux uniform. I wanted his touch on my bare skin. I fucking needed it.

Breaking the kiss, I sucked in a harsh breath as our chests heaved as one against each other.

"Want to get out of here?" I panted.

Memphis groaned deep in his throat and absently

pressed his dick against mine. "You sure? I thought you hated me, which I wouldn't blame you for if you did."

His dark blue eyes blazed with lust, and his voice crackled as if it had been set on fire.

As I really studied Memphis, I realized that what I'd said had been done impulsively in anger, but I hadn't meant it. I wasn't sure I could hate him if I tried, but that didn't mean I was happy about the deception. Horny, yes. Happy, no.

"I don't hate you, Memphis. Don't get me wrong. I'm pissed as hell," I admitted, "but I want this more." And I did. My veins sizzled with the electricity sparking between me and the oversized quarterback. I'd deal with my wishy-washy emotions later, preferably after Memphis fucked me.

Jaw working overtime, his nostrils flared as he loosened his hold, allowing my body to slide down his as I settled onto my feet. His swallow was audible as he nodded. "My place isn't far from here."

I hurriedly stepped back, and surprise rippled through me as Memphis grabbed my hand. He all but dragged me back into the house like a caveman, charging through the thick crowd. I wasn't sure if he even realized what he was doing or even vaguely aware of the eyes that settled on us as he forced a direct path to the door.

"Yo, Memphis..." One of the guys from the team tried to catch his attention, but Memphis was on a one-man mission to get into my pants. He didn't even seem to notice the giant football player who was *creatively* dressed as a football player. "All right then," the guy muttered as he eyed us curiously.

I allowed Memphis to tug me along at a quick clip, and once we made it onto the front lawn, he moved so fast I had to run to keep up.

"Damn, someone's in a hurry," I wheezed as we crossed the street because some of us didn't work out every day. When he slowed, I urged him to get back to the caveman thing he had going on. "I didn't say slow down."

Memphis glanced over his shoulder as he picked up the pace once more. "You have zero idea how much I want you, and I've wanted you for a while."

"Less talking. More moving!" I huffed out. When I really started running and took the lead, Memphis laughed, the deep timbre brushing over my skin in a caress of promises for what he had in store once we made it to his house. I was beyond ready.

We finally made it back to the truck and flung open our doors. The minute my ass touched the leather, Memphis was tugging me over the console. I barely had time to suck in a breath before his mouth covered mine, kissing me impossibly deep. Harder than before and growing in urgency. If he didn't put the pedal to the metal, there was a good chance I'd end up riding his dick in the cab of his truck. Summoning enough willpower for us both, I jerked back. I wanted him behind me, sinking into me so I could feel the power of his big body owning mine. "Get this truck on the road. Now," I ordered.

"Yes, fucking sir." Memphis's lips twitched, but the humor vanished as his gaze dropped to my mouth. "The things I'm going to do to you." He shook his head and started the truck. "Seatbelt. And watch for cops."

"We are the cops," I pointed out as I followed the instruction, whipping the seatbelt over my chest and latching it.

Memphis let out what may have supposed to have been a sigh but instead came out more of a groan. "I swear I'm going to fill that smart mouth of yours with my dick, and then I'm going to fuck your throat."

Like I would say no to that, I mentally scoffed. "Yes, please."

"Fucking pure ass torture," he muttered, repeating himself, as he tore down the street lined with frat houses, his engine becoming a vibrating growl that echoed the rumbling in his throat when he kissed, hungrily, taking what he wanted as if starved. Ten minutes later, he pulled down a country road, tearing down the rough pavement. Headlights reflecting off tall stalks of wheat on either side of the country road, we finally turned down a driveway much sooner than I expected.

A small cabin-style home sat back on what looked like acres of land surrounded by a dense field of tall trees that went on into the dark of night far beyond what I could see.

"You live here?" I asked, surprised. I wasn't sure where I'd pictured Memphis living, but from what I knew about his parents, it wasn't the small, plain rustic home in front of us.

His truck came to a grinding stop on the gravel driveway near the front door.

"Seatbelt." He gritted out the single word as he had before, in a tone that sounded as if barely contained.

"Someone's bossy as hell." Which I liked. "You didn't answer my question."

He simply cocked a brow. "Not what you expected?"

"I'm not sure what I expected," I replied honestly. "But no, not this."

His gaze swung toward the house and back to me. "I don't need much, and I like that out here I can get away from everything whenever I want."

I nodded. Even knowing Memphis came from a wealthy

family, he never acted the part. I realized I loved that about him. He didn't flash his cash around. He didn't even appear to have it in the first place.

"You coming?" he asked as he popped open his door.

"Hopefully multiple times," I quipped, loving the groan that rumbled in his throat.

"Get your ass out of the truck, and I'll make you come until you can't handle it anymore."

Before he could keep issuing orders, and because my dick was so hard it was painful, I scurried down from the truck and followed his long strides as he climbed the steps to the porch. I was suddenly gripped by a strong hand that spun me around. My back collided with Memphis's front door with a thud that ricocheted through my bones, but I barely registered the impact. I didn't even care. Especially when he pinned me in place, grinding his cock into my belly, replacing the slight pain with a burn that wrapped my body in invisible flames that threatened to scorch us both into a pile of ash if he didn't give me what I needed to tame the blaze. Him. Inside me.

Memphis ripped his lips from mine, gasping. "I saw you watching me last year. It wasn't one-sided. There was never a time when I didn't notice you, Tristan. Fucking never. Even when I tried to, you were always there, taunting me with what I thought I couldn't have."

What would have happened if I hadn't confronted him that night? I'd never have known how badly I'd affected him. In a good way as far as I was concerned. If he didn't let us inside soon, I was going to pass out from lack of blood flow that insisted on pulsing in my too-tight pants.

"You can have me if you open this door." I stepped aside, and Memphis cursed, darting forward, unlocking the door with a click that hit me like a bolt of lightning.

This was happening. *Holy shit*, this was happening.

Memphis shoved the door open, grabbed my hand and hauled me inside before kicking the door closed. Giving me no time to inspect his space, he headed for a hallway, tugging me with him.

I went willingly, only stopping when we entered his room, and he suddenly let go of my hand. He paused, swallowing hard as he faced me before blowing out a deep breath. "Fuck, I want you so damn bad. I need you naked and beneath me."

Eyes blazing a path over my body, he worked to free the buttons of the police costume, popping off a few in the process. His skin glowed in the pale blue moonlight slipping through the open blinds. Inch by tempting inch, he exposed a toned chest, and I took him in, trembling at the sight.

Lifting my gaze, I stared into those deep intense blue eyes, hooded as they watched me steadily with single-minded focus as if I was the only thing that mattered. I expected a smirk. A *like what you see?* line. Instead, Memphis closed the space between us, lifting his hands to deftly work my buttons free in a practiced move while never breaking eye contact. "Tristan," he whispered. "I have never needed anything as badly as I need you right now."

I didn't know what to say. Memphis was voicing my own thoughts. I wondered if he could possibly be experiencing the same need that coursed through my veins as my cock grew harder than it ever had before. This was happening. Memphis would be buried inside of me soon when, only weeks ago, I'd thought he didn't know I existed. But Memphis had been the guy I owed my confidence to. He was the one who'd unknowingly changed my life with a reassuring presence and dusting of his lips against mine. The stranger who had always been on my mind. I was an idiot. Two people couldn't own that smile. Those dimples. His voice. Now that I knew he'd been the stranger, I couldn't believe I'd ever convinced myself otherwise.

I shivered as Memphis slid the thin fabric away from my shoulders, bending to brush his lips along my shoulder while tracing his tongue up to gently suck my neck. My knees shook, dangerously close to buckling altogether. "I need out of this thing. Now," I rasped.

He pulled away, tearing at his own clothes as I peeled away mine. Naked and bare before me, Memphis looked like a Greek statue—a sculpture of pure art. Chiseled muscles from hard workouts made my fingers flex with the urge to touch him. His hard length was longer and thicker than mine, making my mouth water with the need to taste him. He didn't give me much time to gawk as he scooped me up before tossing me onto the soft mattress of his huge bed, as if I weighed nothing. I hit the cushioned top, sinking down as he crawled over me where he stilled, staring down at me. Our eyes laser-focused on each other.

"Memphis, I'm going to need you to fuck me." I wasn't beyond begging, and he must have read the desperation on my face. I wasn't sure he realized it likely mirrored his own.

Curses spilled from his mouth, and his lips came down hard on mine. His tongue dove deep, entwining with mine. The slick slide drove me crazy, and the sensation only heightened when he lowered his body, pressing his weight against me, sinking us further into the bed.

Memphis pulled back with a gasping breath. "You drive me crazy. So fucking insane."

My gaze latched onto his lips before they kissed their way down my body as he scooted off the bed, pausing as he hovered over my dick that rested hard against my stomach. His ragged breathing sent bursts of air that coasted over my cock, making it twitch in response. I wasn't sure how much more I could handle before I begged him to touch me. To stop the torture of the teasing sensation.

"Fuck," he whispered reverently as he swiped his tongue over my pierced tip, flicking the silver hoop slowly. "I've thought about tonguing the fuck out of this piercing so many damn times."

My legs jerked, and I was just about to protest any type of foreplay to speed things along when Memphis angled my dick and sucked it straight to the back of his throat. "Fuck. Shit. Holy..." A litany of unintelligible words fell from my lips as he worked me with a skilled mouth that made my sac draw tight. I did not want to come yet. Not before I had him buried balls deep in my ass. "Stop. Memphis, *stop*."

Letting my dick fall free from his mouth, he glanced up at me with an almost feral gaze. "What do you need, babe?"

"Condom and lube." I squeezed the base of my dick to keep my orgasm at bay.

Memphis's jaw clenched before he jerked back, stood, reached for the side table and yanked it open so hard I swore I heard the wood splinter.

Mute, I watched as he ripped open the foil with his teeth and rolled the rubber down his hard length. I swallowed hard as he flicked open the cap of the lube and slicked his shaft, stroking himself in the process. A moan stuck in my throat, and I shifted restlessly, staring at his hand sliding up and down.

"Keep moving that tight little body like that, and you're going to get fucked hard." Memphis reached down and cupped his sac, massaging and tugging at the skin. He liked his balls played with. Happily noted.

My brow furrowed at the *threat*. "Is that seriously supposed to stop me?"

To prove my point, I rolled to my stomach and lifted up on all fours, spreading my legs and lowering onto my forearms. I knew what I looked like. Ass exposed, inviting him to look, touch, taste, or fuck. Usually, I didn't care in what order, but right now..."Fuck me."

Heavy breathing filled the otherwise quiet bedroom. "You are fucking perfect," Memphis murmured as he tossed the lube on the bed and urged me forward to make room for him. Behind me, he settled between my legs, resting back on his calves and gripped a cheek in each massive hand, spreading them farther apart. "Such a tight little ass. You want my dick here, Tris?"

The rough pad of his lubed thumb brushed over my asshole, and I bit my arm to muffle the moan. I nodded and received a sharp swat to my ass. "Yes!" I yelped.

He hummed in approval, returning to touching me where I wanted him most. "So, you like to be fucked hard?"

"By you? Yes. I want to feel it tomorrow. I want it to burn for days." And I did. For the next week, every time I sat, I wanted to be reminded of this night because I had no idea if it would happen again. What would happen in the light of day? Would he regret it? I knew I wouldn't.

Memphis's groan met my moan when he unexpectedly sank a thick finger into me with one slick slide, making me clench around him. He worked me open, back and forth, drawing out sounds from my throat I wasn't even aware I could make. Dizzy ecstasy swirled in my brain as he added a second finger and then a third. His long, skilled fingers stretched me in a way I'd never experienced, eliciting a trail of precome onto the bedspread. "I'm sort of making a mess here," I moaned.

"Good. I want you messy, dirty, and begging. You going to do that for me, Tris?" Memphis picked up the pace, scissoring his fingers, prepping me to take his fat cock. "Tell me how bad you want it."

"Jesus, you dirty talking bastard. Fuck me already." If he didn't, he was going to find himself knocked on his ass while I rode his dick anyway. I didn't care how big and heavy he was. I was *gone*.

Memphis chuckled, dark and low, before I felt the bed dip as he rose onto his knees behind me, pressing his tip to my asshole. One of his rough hands gripped my shoulder while the other one held his dick steady. And then he pushed forward, stuffing me full as he inched his way inside of me. A long, drawn-out moan melted between my lips, and I became boneless as he brushed over the sensitive patch that had been overstimulated by his talented fingers. I wouldn't last long. The only thing holding me up was the strong grip Memphis had on my shoulder, while he skated the other hand over my skin to my hip, holding me in place as he sank balls deep.

Draping himself over my back, Memphis whispered next to my ear, "Baby, breathe." I hadn't realized I'd been holding my breath, and it came out in a rush of air. He nipped my earlobe, humming, "That's better." Then he pulled back, a slow drag that tore a desperate moan from my throat before pushing into me again with an unhurried pace. Memphis's groan was straight out of a wet dream, a gravelly sound that sounded as if it had been dragged through a bed of broken glass. "Fuck, you're so damn tight. So fucking good."

I managed a muffled agreement that was cut off when he really began to fuck me. Hard, like he'd promised. My eyes rolled back, my world boiling down to the dizzying sensation of Memphis moving inside of me, stretching me with the steady glide of his cock pumping in and out, forcing my orgasm to race down my spine.

"Memphis," I mumbled as the pressure in my balls grew too much. Reaching beneath me, I jerked my dick to the sound of his deep groans. "I'm so going to come."

"Fuck yeah. Touch yourself. Come for me," Memphis growled as his hand came down on my ass with a surprising sting, and it was over for me. My legs shook as I went hurtling over the edge, striping the dark comforter in ribbons of sticky come. "Next time," Memphis grunted as his thrusts became erratic, "I want you on your back. I want to see you come, and I want you covered in mine."

Next time. The phrase brought a fresh wave of ecstasy rolling through my body, and I clenched, ripping a growl from Memphis's chest. Once. Twice. He thrust into me with a force that jolted me forward before he stilled on the third, his grip tightening and digging into my skin as he came deep inside me. Spent, he sagged forward, heaving chest against my back. I couldn't support his weight and fell onto my stomach. Lifting slightly to let me breathe, Memphis rained down soft kisses along the side of my neck and then down my spine, which tingled at the brush of his lips as he crawled off the bed.

"Let's go clean up." I heard him rifling through his dresser drawer but couldn't make myself get up. He laughed from behind me. "Would it be more persuasive if I told you I planned to clean your dick with my mouth?"

"There is no way my dick is getting hard again any time soon," I assured him, cracking my eyes open just enough to look at him. I wasn't even sure I'd be able to stand upright in a shower at the moment, much less expect my dick to rally.

Memphis gave me a wicked grin. "We'll see about that. I still want to play with that dick piercing."

My gaze flicked to his groin. "Are you sporting a fucking semi already?"

"Not for long." His gaze wove a lazy path down my nude body.

I watched him, impressed as hell as he continued to harden. I was also a little insulted. "I guess I'll have to work harder to wear you out."

He shook his head slowly. "As long as I've waited for this? It's going to be a while before the sight of you lying naked doesn't get my dick hard. Just fucked or not."

"Help me up." I managed to roll onto my back and held my hands out to him.

Gripping my wrists, he tugged me to my feet. Surprisingly sweet, he dipped and gave me a soft kiss. "You drive me so fucking crazy. In both good and bad ways."

My lips quirked into a grin. I was supposed to be livid, dammit. Post orgasm, I was supposed to remember he was a lying jerkface. But with his dimples deepening as his smile matched mine, I remembered the man in front of me was the same man who had stolen a part of my heart the night he'd given me my first kiss. I hadn't even realized it until that moment.

I scowled. "Liar *and* a thief."

His smile dropped, and brows rose. "Um, what?"

Like he didn't know he kept stealing stuff from me. A kiss. And now a piece of my heart. I held back the annoyed snort as I circled around him and headed for the bathroom. "I was promised a blowjob."

"It's a good thing I'm used to you not making a lot of sense," he muttered behind me and then turned on the shower. And then Memphis made good on his promise, on his knees sucking the fuck out of my dick. He really was obsessed with my piercing, not that I was complaining.

THIRTEEN

TRISTAN

MEMPHIS WAS DEAD WEIGHT, squashing me for the second morning in a row. Who knew he'd be like a sloth, wrapping himself around me like a damn cuddly critter—which I guess made me the skinny tree branch. The first night we hooked up was spent at his house. The next morning had been a frenzy of him rushing to get ready for practice before the sun had even risen so he could take me home first. After a day of classes and both morning and afternoon practices, Memphis had shown up at my apartment uninvited, with his bag of spare clothes and practice gear in hand. I hadn't exactly turned him away. Freshly showered and with a dirty smile in place, he'd dropped his shit next to the door and practically sank to his knees on the spot. Call me crazy, but I'd decided he was welcome to stay.

Now? My slick skin covered in sweat from his body heat was pissed about it. I shoved his shoulder. "Wake up, you heavy behemoth."

"Huh?" He blinked open sleepy blue eyes, the color of the ocean at dusk, grinning when they focused on me. I had to force myself not to smile back because a massive football player was suffocating me again.

"I can't breathe," I wheezed and pushed at him again. "And you feel as hot as a freaking dragon's breath furnace."

"Shit, sorry." Memphis rolled off of me with a yawn, and I sucked in a deep breath as my lungs were finally able to expand. "What time is it?"

Based on a sliver of pale morning sunlight curling around the window curtains... "Like seven or something, I think. How much do you weigh?" I squinted at his naked body in annoyance. My dick, on the other hand, decided to betray me as my morning wood throbbed at the sight of miles of lightly bronzed, slightly freckled skin. In the light of day, the birthmark low on his stomach would have given him away even if he hadn't admitted to being my skittish app friend that day.

"Fuck!" Memphis's gravelly shout shook me from staring at his ridiculous body. He jumped off the bed like his ass was on fire. "I'm late for practice."

Propping myself up on my elbows, I watched as he hurried around my room, scooping up his discarded clothes from the night before. His black boxer briefs covered the fun stuff, so I was able to pay attention again. "Are you going to be in trouble?"

"Probably." After digging through his bag, Memphis slipped into a pair of shorts even though I knew it would be at least somewhat cold outside. "Coach may make me stay late or watch extra film. Who knows? Depends on his mood."

"Can't you just tell them you got plenty of exercise last night?" I mean, it was true.

"If sex was a good excuse to miss the torture of practice,

most of the team would never show up." A devilish grin spread over his lush lips, giving me a peek at those dimples. The same dimples that should have given him away as the stranger I'd thought about so many times. Instead, I'd subconsciously developed a crush on a mystery man I hadn't recognized as Memphis. Probably because he'd been a dick to me on campus.

I dropped back on to the bed, rolling on my side to face him as he slid a wrinkled black sleeveless shirt over his head. Even with sleep rumpled dark hair, and sort of a total mess, he was too hot for his own good. "Yeah, well, they aren't having sex with me, so they can't really compare that kind of workout."

"Tristan," Memphis growled, sitting on the side of the bed closest to me as he shoved on his shoes. "If I tell them how good you are in bed, they might try to steal you away from me. And I'm nowhere close to being done with you."

I cocked my head, mulling over that possibility. "Good point."

Memphis shook his head while chuckling, then leaned down, popping a quick kiss on my lips. "See you tonight."

"That's a bit presumptuous." I scowled at the cocky jock who thought getting in my pants was now an all-access pass.

His lips tipped at one side as he agreed. "Yeah. It is."

I glared, but Memphis only smiled wider before strolling out of my room.

When I heard the front door close behind him, I bit my lip while considering whether or not to meet up with him tonight. Maybe I just wouldn't answer the door at all. Nope. I wasn't going to let the cocksure bastard back in my apartment. With a solid nod to myself, I glanced at the clock on my phone.

"This is why being an athlete is stupid," I mumbled aloud before I closed my eyes. "Ass crack of dawn..." I yawned as sleep dragged me back into its loving arms. "Fuck that."

I WAS TOTALLY GOING to open the door for Memphis. Class was boring as hell, and I could really use something to make my day better. Namely, his thick dick and ridiculously talented mouth. The rest of him could tag along, I supposed, because it would be creepy as shit if not.

Professor Morton was droning on about the importance of nutrition. I was required to take Fundamentals of Nutrition as a general ed course, but other than avoiding alcohol, I couldn't say I did much to ensure the right vitamins and food groups were introduced to my body each day. Nor did I care, especially since his monotone voice was void of enthusiasm for his chosen field of expertise.

I was interested in the mind. Not the body... mostly. Though I was assured those two things went hand and hand, I wasn't sold yet. Hamburgers, fries, and strawberry milkshakes made me happy. Couldn't argue with personal research.

Instead, I found myself distracted and completely immersed in thoughts of Memphis as they often were. On one hand, I still felt betrayed. On the other, he had been the catalyst for me owning who I was when I had been on the verge of drowning in humiliation. Now? No fucks given, thanks to the stranger who'd understood me. The one who had sat next to me while I was a complete mess and comforted me when he hadn't known me at all.

How could I not have recognized those dimples? I'd been so blind. I shook my head slightly. It was the same barrage of questions I seemed to have every time we separated.

I wasn't mad, exactly. His explanation had made sense, even if I didn't love the situation. Honestly, it made me feel *seen* even when I thought he was completely oblivious to my existence last year. Turned out, I had been far from invisible to him, and that knowledge brought a small stupid grin to my face.

I'd picked up the phone several times to call Rendon to fill him in on everything that had happened since I'd found out he'd also been keeping the secret from me that Memphis was into guys, but I'd hesitated each time I went to dial his number. I wasn't sure what Memphis had told Nash, and I knew Rendon would repeat everything I said word for word to his boyfriend. There was also the fact that hanging out and banging out were two totally different things, and I wasn't sure what Memphis was comfortable telling people.

My professor's voice penetrated my musings. "It is imperative to account for physical activity when—"

I get plenty of physical activity, I thought, before too easily tuning him out once again. Fishing my phone from my pocket, I texted Memphis.

Me: *Fine. Bring your presumptuous ass over.*

The response was immediate.

Captain Jock-o-potamus: *Already planned to.*

I scowled because... well, just because Memphis was being Memphis.

Me: *Aren't you supposed to be in class?*

Captain Jock-o-potamus: *Just got out and headed to the athletic building. What about you?*

I glanced up at my professor, who was giving a limp point toward a graph on the projector.

Me: *I am, but I'm bored.*

Captain Jock-o-potamus: *I'll fix that tonight. ;) I have to go. See you in a few hours.*

Sighing, I stuffed my phone back in my pocket. We were good together in bed. He'd wormed his way into becoming my new best, annoying friend. But one thing I was uncertain of was where Memphis and I stood now that the truth had come out and we'd slept together. Were we still just friends? Did I want to be more? My brow furrowed as I considered the possibility because I'd never had a boyfriend. I didn't want to share Memphis. At all. Ever. Nor did hooking up with anyone else appeal to me.

But did he want more out of our maybe-relationship? Would I be capable of having a relationship with someone who would hide me from everyone?

Impulsively, I dug my phone back out of my pocket and tapped out another text.

Me: *So, are we like dating now?*

I frowned at the message but hit send anyway. I needed things to be clear so I could set my expectations accordingly.

When my phone didn't vibrate with an answer, I stuffed it back in my pocket and proceeded to try to gain enough information to at least pass this stupid class and then hunt down a juicy burger and fries just to spite the lesson. Plus, I needed a distraction. Hopefully, Memphis hadn't seen the text. Because if he had and didn't answer, that could only mean I was on an island all my own. Memphis may want my body, but a relationship?

Maybe I shouldn't have sent the stupid text. He'd be busy with practice, and I still had two classes to sit through. Too much time to stew over his answer. I thought about texting him back, telling him to forget it. Create some elaborate story to make it go away. But in the end, the simple fact was that I *needed* to know.

I slumped in my chair, doing my best to pay attention, but now finding it was impossible.

PRACTICE WAS ROUGH AS HELL, but not because Coach made me pay for being late this morning. He hadn't done more than give me a warning, likely because I looked like shit. My lack of sleep over the last few nights had me dragging ass out on the field. Some of my teammates noticed my low energy level, causing them to question me at both practice sessions today.

With eyelids drooping, I wrapped a towel around my waist—a pointless exercise—and made my way around my smelly teammates before untying it to step beneath an available showerhead.

"Late night or what?" Logan asked from the space beside me as he lathered his hair with some expensive smelling shampoo.

I soaped my body as I nodded. "Something like that."

He chuckled. "Who is she?"

My hand paused over my chest briefly before I resumed cleaning up. *No one* wasn't true, but the question caught me off guard. It didn't feel right to pretend I'd been with a girl when I'd really been with Tristan. So, I settled on a vague answer. "You don't know them."

"'Them? As in more than one?" Logan asked, obviously impressed.

I glanced at him. "Negative."

One Tristan was more than enough, as evidenced by yet another yawn that crept up my throat.

Logan chuckled. "Well, I'd ask if it was Tristan since you seem to be up his ass lately, but since you're not gay... "

I flinched slightly and was relieved when I saw he had his eyes closed, rinsing the shampoo away. "Why are you interested in my sex life? Don't you still have a boyfriend?"

His eyes popped open, and he frowned. "You know I do. It was just a joke, man. What's up with you?"

Shaking my head, I finished washing the soap away. "Nothing. Sorry. I usually give you more shit than that. I'm just tired." *And paranoid, apparently.*

"It's cool." He studied me. "You do look like you haven't slept in a week."

I snorted. "Thanks, dick."

I snagged my towel, tying it around my waist and exited the stall before he could say anything else. Joke or not, he'd been more correct than he knew, and I hadn't known how to respond. Popping open my locker, I grabbed my clothes and slowly got dressed. I wasn't sure I had the energy to go another round with Tristan. Honestly, I just wanted to climb in his bed and go the fuck to sleep.

After shoving my feet into my shoes, I checked my phone for the time and saw I had a text waiting from Tristan. I clicked it.

Tristan: *So, are we like dating now?*

A shot of adrenaline spiked my blood, and my heart

pounded as I reread the message. *Dating?* I swallowed around the rapidly developing ball of panic building in my throat. *Were Tristan and I dating?* Maybe on some level, I just assumed we were, but I hadn't put any sort of label on it. Of course, I had no intention of sharing him. So deep down, I knew what that meant. The sudden need to label our relationship caught me off guard, and right after Logan's offhand remark, it was a double dose of being put on the spot.

There was no way I could say no. That would be a lie. But was I ready to say yes? I checked the time he'd sent the text and scrubbed a hand over my jaw. Tristan had sent the message right after I'd thrown my phone in my locker and headed out to the practice field. Who knew what was going through his eccentric brain on a regular basis, much less after sending something like that. And what was I supposed to say now? There were too many guys around, and I couldn't think.

After I zipped up my bag, I pulled it over my shoulder and headed toward the door.

"Get some sleep tonight, Hale," Logan yelled over the noise.

I gave an absent nod and dragged myself out to my truck. Sitting in the cab, I tapped out a quick response to Tristan.

Me: *Sorry, I just got your text. You home yet?*
Tristan: *Yep.*

One word. For Tristan, that was enough to tell me he wasn't happy. I needed the few minutes it would take to drive to his place to think.

Me: *I'm headed over.*

Nash was the only person that knew I swung both ways, so even though I really wasn't up to listening to his inevitable rant when I told him about Tristan, he was the only person I could talk to about it. I would have to take the chance he wouldn't spill to Rendon who would tell Tristan how confused I was. Bluetooth automatically connected after I started the truck. "Call Nash."

The phone rang as I pulled away from the athletic complex.

"'Sup?" Nash's smooth voice came over the speakers.

I hesitated. "Rendon around?"

"No, I'm just leaving the facility, and he's at work." Nash paused. "Why?"

My fingers tapped a nervous rhythm on the wheel. "I need to talk to you."

"About Rendon?" He sounded perplexed, and I shook my head even though he couldn't see it.

I let out a sigh and turned onto the down ramp to hop on the highway. "No... About Tristan."

Silence met my comment. "Dude, no. You're fucking Tristan?"

"It's not like that," I snapped.

"No?" Nash's tone held a bite I rarely heard, definitely not directed at me anyway.

I tensed. "I said it's not, and it's not."

"Fine. What's it like?"

"Tristan..." I licked my lips as I considered how to approach the topic. "Yes, we are fucking. But not *just* fucking. I like him."

Nash let out a reluctant chuckle. "You like him. Tristan Stafford? Emo twink."

"You deaf?" I asked, which only made him laugh louder. "Shut up, dick. He asked if we were dating."

His laughter stopped as suddenly as it had started. "Are you?"

"I'm not sleeping with anyone else. Pretty sure he's not

either." I paused. "But dating? How am I supposed to date him when no one knows I even like guys?"

Nash hummed. "Well, I guess the first question is, do you want to be a thing with him?"

I nodded before remembering he couldn't see me and cleared my throat. "I mean, yeah. It's just... I don't know how that's possible."

"Tristan knows you're not out, so why don't you leave what he's comfortable with up to him," Nash suggested as if it was that easy.

That was the problem. "And if he's not cool with being on the d.l.? Do I just walk away? What if he does?"

"Damn. It's like *that*." Nash resumed laughing. "Dick whipped!"

"Nash," I growled. I was running out of time before I'd be at Tristan's apartment. "Seriously."

"I am serious, dick. If you're so worried he'll bail, which, I'm not going to lie, could happen, you need to decide which risk is higher. I keep telling you coming out will be fine. I'm not going to say that shit's all roses because it's not. But I'm bisexual. That's my life and my business. And there's not a chance in hell I'd keep Rendon a secret. But I already wasn't keeping my shit quiet. If you're thinking about doing it for Tristan... aren't you moving kind of fast?"

"You literally have no room to talk considering how shit went down with Rendon." Nash didn't know the full truth about how long ago I'd met Tristan. There was nothing fast about what was happening between us. I wasn't sure how to even tell him, and it wasn't my story to tell anyway.

Nash let out a long sigh. "What is it you want me to tell you, Memphis? You want the little dude or not?"

"Yes." That answer was easy enough.

"Question. Now that all of this fuckery is going on, did

you really not notice him last year?" I groaned, and Nash laughed. "You did, didn't you?"

"Does it matter?" Tristan's exit came into view, and my heart rate increased. "This has not been helpful."

Nash huffed an exasperated breath. "Look, it's simple. You're either willing to risk your career, or you're willing to risk losing Tristan. The former isn't going to happen just because you're boning a dude, especially with your talent, despite your worries. The latter... like I said, that's on you."

Exiting the highway, I mulled over what Nash was saying. "This is exactly why I don't date."

"Except that you do now," Nash unhelpfully pointed out. "Where's the lie?"

Nowhere. "I have a boyfriend, I think."

"Yeah," he agreed. "Which is weird on its own, but I think I already had an idea something was going on when you two started hanging out."

I pulled into the parking lot of the apartment complex. "I'm at his place, so I gotta run. Thanks for the pep talk or whatever."

"Good luck." Nash chuckled.

I disconnected the call as I pulled into an empty space. Fatigue settled heavily in my bones as I locked the truck and headed for the stairs.

After knocking, I stepped back and shoved my hands in my pockets as I waited. When Tristan opened the door, he took one look at me and stepped aside. "They punish you for being late this morning?"

"Nah." I stepped inside and kicked off my shoes as he closed the door. "Just tired. *Someone* hasn't let me sleep much this week."

I turned for the bedroom, and as soon as the bed came into view, I let out a sigh of relief and collapsed face first.

"You're staying?" Tristan asked, sounding surprised.

I pried my eyelids open, and I swear it felt like sandpaper. "Unless you don't want me to."

"No, it's fine. After your text... I really wasn't sure... " He trailed off, lifting one shoulder.

"Come here." I crooked a finger, and he slid onto the bed, lying next to me. "You want to know if we're dating?"

He shrugged as if he didn't care. Sometimes Tristan was hard to read, but he was clearly lying when he said, "Nah, totally doesn't matter. I was just curious." He paused. "It's just weird because we hated each other—"

I interrupted him. "I never hated you."

He ignored me completely. "And then you forced me to be your best friend. And then obviously we had sex because you couldn't keep your huge paws off the merchandise. So now I'm not sure if we're friends with benefits..."

"Tristan." I stopped him, twining my fingers through his. "I'm not fucking anyone else. I'm not seeing anyone else. And I sure as fuck hope you're not either." Wait. *Friends with benefits?* I frowned. "You want to be friends with benefits?"

"That's not what I said. It was simply an option." He lifted one shoulder casually.

The fuck it is. "Not for me, it isn't."

Gnawing on his lip, Tristan cocked a brow. "Sooo..."

"Sooo," I repeated, fighting to keep my eyes open.

"Oh my god," Tristan snapped. "Tell me already. "

"What? That we're dating? I thought I just said that."

"You didn't just say that, Memphis Hale." A vee formed between his eyebrows. "You know I've never had a boyfriend, right? I may suck at it."

"I hope so." I wiggled my eyebrows, and he snorted. "But same for me, so fair warning."

"I hope so," he mimicked me with the same move of his brow, bringing a tired grin to my face.

"I want to sleep for the next week." Forcing myself to roll over, I worked my way up the bed until I lay comfortably on my back with a pillow beneath my head. "At least my boyfriend has a comfortable bed, but it's too small. Tomorrow night, my house."

"You may have to say that like five thousand times before it sinks in." Tristan gave me a dopey grin I matched.

"Boyfriend?" He hummed a yes, and I totally understood because it would take time for me to get used to it as well. "I told Nash," I admitted. "I needed his advice, and he's the only one, other than you and Rendon, who knows I'm bi." I waited to see if Tristan would be mad.

He only sighed. "Nash is going to tell Rendon."

"You don't want him to?"

Tristan shook his head. "Nah, it's fine. I just really wanted to see his face. Pretty sure he's going to be mad I didn't talk to him, but I wasn't sure if you were ready for that."

"I should have asked you first." Memphis frowned.

"Whatever. I don't care who tells him. As far as I'm concerned you belong to me. My own personal beanstalk giant." I didn't even question his claim on me, because it was true. He paused and I studied him. "I deleted the app today."

I stiffened, narrowing my tired eyes. "You just deleted it today?"

"I didn't think about it before because I haven't even turned it on since we met, or from the day I *thought* we met."

A satisfied grin slanted my lips.

Tristan scowled. "This is where you say you deleted it too."

"Oh, I did. But unlike you, I did it after the away game when I called you. I knew then I wouldn't use it again. Not while I couldn't stop thinking about you. The idea of the thing on my phone at all bothered me."

"Good. But I really just didn't think about it until today."

I lifted an arm. "Enough about the stupid app. Come here."

Tristan scooted into the space next to me and awkwardly rested his head on my chest. "Stop being weird," I scolded him.

"I think that's like asking Medusa to stop turning shit into stone. Pretty sure that bitch is never gonna let that happen." I laughed but sighed when Tristan relaxed. "Besides, it doesn't matter what I do. The minute your eyes close, you're going to go all sloth on me and suffocate me with your gigantic arms."

"You like it," I accused with a grin, tilting my head to take a deep inhale of his cinnamon shampoo.

"What I like is *breathing*." Tristan snorted.

Humming in contentment when he wiggled closer, I hugged him tight.

"Here we go again," he muttered with an exasperated huff.

OUR PROFESSOR STOOD at his desk, rearranging papers as the stadium-style classroom buzzed with the sound of students chatting while everyone gathered their things and made a beeline for the door.

My next class was the dreaded health lecture on what substances should and should not be put in our bodies to aid a healthy mind. Not a fan of the course, I moved slower than most until I was the last to leave.

On my way out, I paused when my phone buzzed in my pocket and dug it free. I hoped to see my boyfriend's name on the screen—which still boggled my mind that I was dating the Saints' quarterback. How the hell had that happened? The story we'd tell, or at least I would, would be that it started the traditional way. *Boy meets jock. Jock changes the boy's life and then ends up lying before hopelessly falling in love with the boy. After being kidnapped, of course, by said jock.* Disappointed, I saw it was only my dad.

I had to give my overprotective parents credit, though. They hadn't checked in yesterday. They were at least attempting to loosen the reins a bit. I answered the call.

"Hey, Dad." I leaned against the white-painted cement blocks that lined the hallway.

"Tristan," he acknowledged in a rough voice that already told me he was worried. I held back a sigh. Some people had parents that didn't care at all. I was lucky. "We just wanted to check in and see how things are going."

"They're good. Just got out of class, and I'm on my way to the next one." And would be late if I didn't get moving.

"I'm glad to hear that." He breathed out a sigh of relief, and I rubbed my finger against my eye. It had just occurred to me that I'd have to tell my parents about Memphis if things worked out between us. I had no idea how they'd take the news. They definitely weren't aware of my private activities. I could only imagine the shock they'd feel when I told them it had been Memphis who'd been responsible for removing Brantley from school. How he'd done that, I still wasn't sure. I made a mental note to ask him. Dad continued, "We are planning a visit next weekend. Are you free Saturday?"

Saturday. *Shit.* Another realization popped into place. Would I have to go to Memphis's games? I mean, it wouldn't be a hardship to watch him play, in the uniform that made a bit of drool gather at the corners of my mouth. But I could always ask him to wear it for me privately instead... *No.* I shook my head. I'd support him by showing up because I was a selfless human, sacrificing the comfort of my ass to the uncomfortable seats of the stadium. It would be the first game I attended as the other half of a couple. If I wanted to show Memphis I was serious, I'd need to go. "Actually. Saturday isn't great."

"No?" He sounded surprised, which made sense because I'd always been able to adjust my non-existent social schedule before. I considered lying, but my mouth, as usual, just decided things for me. "My boyfriend has a big game that day, and I'm pretty sure I'm supposed to be there."

Silence met my admission, and I counted the seconds in my head, waiting for the inevitable meltdown through the line.

"Boyfriend?" my mom asked with shock and worry shaking her voice. I wasn't surprised at all that she'd been listening in on the call.

I cleared my throat. "Yeah. Weird, right?"

"He's an athlete." My dad inferred from context as his voice roughened. "Tristan—"

"He's nothing like Brantley," I assured them, meaning it from deep within my soul. Memphis wasn't like anyone else I'd ever known.

"How well do you know him?" my mom asked.

Actually, I had a lot to learn about Memphis, but I knew that answer would only make my parents uneasy. "He's a good guy. The best, actually. He's thoughtful... Listen, guys. I think you'd really like him if you gave him a chance. But it's new."

A muffled sigh came through the phone. "We worry."

No kidding. "So, it's kinda weird, though. What happened in high school—the anonymous caller. It was him."

"Tristan, how would you possibly know that? You don't know who made that call." My dad immediately rebuffed the story.

After briefly explaining what had happened between Memphis and me that night—some of the facts they'd already known—but leaving out the kiss, they reluctantly accepted what I told them was true. I knew my dad would at least do his best to fact-check, though.

"You like him." My mom hesitated. "Do you love him?"

Love him? Did I? How would I know if I did? Memphis annoyed me a lot but in the best way. He also made me smile, and a weird shot of electricity made my heart pound when he was near. But love? "Like I said, it's new."

"Okay." My mom breathed out and repeated more clearly, "Okay, then. Does Sunday work?"

"Sunday is fine," I assured them. "Maybe you can meet him then."

I immediately thought that maybe I should have asked Memphis first, but the damage was done. Once again, I cursed my non-existent impulse control.

"We'll see you this weekend. Hopefully, you can introduce us to your boyfriend," Mom said. Dad had been quiet, and I knew he'd struggle with the situation more than my mom.

We briefly talked about school, and I was already so late for class that I planned on skipping. But if I had rushed them off the phone, I knew they'd sit around, stressing until I called them back. I couldn't and wouldn't do that to them.

When we said our goodbyes, I headed for the front door of the building, drawing up short when the last person I expected to see greeted me. Looking all kinds of hot, Memphis leaned casually against the brick column. He wore a pair of stonewash jeans with a rip at one knee and a dark blue hoodie. His dark hair curled up around the edges of his dingy white baseball cap that he wore turned backward. Dimples deep from the grin that spread over his face once he saw me, he held out a strawberry milkshake. I swear my knees wobbled as I took in the sight of my two favorite things. I was confident in the way I looked, but how the fuck had I bagged this sex on a stick cum drainer, who was also apparently super sweet?

Biting my lip, I stepped forward and reached for the

shake. "You trying to get in my pants, stalker? I mean, this *is* the way to do it." I took a long draw from the frothy pink perfection.

"That would just be a bonus." He winked, appearing much more rested today. "Can't I just come see you? That's part of my new job description, right?"

"Correct," I agreed because strawberry milkshakes were definitely a rule. "How'd you know where to find me?"

"There's never been a time when I didn't know where to find you." He wiggled his brows.

"That was vaguely creepy." I cocked a brow, and he laughed.

"Always crossing paths, remember? I told you I noticed and even paid attention." Memphis sobered, and a warm glow lit my chest. Or something similarly sappy. Sappy warmth, I decided.

"I hadn't realized you'd been taking notes." I grinned when he laughed again. My favorite sound. But I didn't really know what my next move should be—how to show my appreciation, or greet him in general. Especially when we headed down the campus sidewalk, I assumed in the direction of my next class since Memphis apparently knew my schedule. How comfortable was he in public about our relationship? I could ask myself the same question. "Won't you be late to class?"

He made a face as if he was insulted. "You haven't been paying attention as much as you claimed if you don't know that I have a gap between class and practice today."

"I told myself after last year when you were *ignoring* me to ignore you back. I was somewhat successful." More so than him, it would seem, and I mentally patted myself on the back for the solid effort I'd given.

"But you're already late," he pointed out as he shifted his

backpack strap on his shoulder. "I was beginning to wonder if you hadn't gone to class at all after everyone else left."

"My parents called," I explained. "They are a little overprotective after everything that happened in high school, so I had to answer. I didn't want them to freak out."

Memphis didn't question what I'd said, only nodding in response. I held my milkshake in one hand, letting the other one dangle close to his. Carrying his bookbag on his shoulder, Memphis had a free hand too. As we walked, the back of our hands brushed against each other, sending a tingling feeling through my fingers. I was still deciding if it had been on purpose when he hooked his pinky around mine. Ducking my head, I hid my smile. No need for him to know how much that small connection meant to me. Once I gathered my composure again, I lifted my head. "Anyway, since I'm already beyond late, I'm skipping."

"Such a bad boy," he scolded, and when I glanced at him, his eyes twinkled with amusement.

"Officer Hale, are you going to punish me?" I bit my lip suggestively.

Memphis groaned. "That shit right there is going to get you fucked."

I hummed. "If I remember correctly, the last time you threatened that I gladly let you."

"Shit," he muttered before he snatched my hand and then marched toward the closest building—the math department.

A few students were milling around the quad, so the move surprised me. I hadn't realized he'd be jumping right into this whole public thing. Brows raised, I moved quickly, keeping up with his long strides. When we entered, he stepped quietly, scanning the empty hall. "This way," he said as he pulled me along the corridor and pressed open the door to a... janitor's closet.

The scent of diluted bleach filled the air, and the small space was filled with wire racks that held towels and other cleaning supplies. Closing the door, Memphis flipped on the dim light.

"Damn, *someone* knew where this was way too quickly." I scowled, and he took my cup, setting it on a rack behind me.

"Shut up. I've never fucked anyone anywhere on campus." He gripped my chin, tilting it upward, making me stare him in the eyes.

"Really?" I furrowed my brow because Memphis had girls chasing his nuts daily, not that he ever seemed to notice them.

"You have." His jaw set, and I *almost* let him squirm. But he'd been so sweet I couldn't.

"Nope," I answered truthfully.

His nostrils flared. "Good."

I laughed, cocking a brow. "And if I had?"

"Then I would have had to burn all of the places down." His tone lacked humor, and my brows climbed high.

"That escalated to psychotic very quickly." I grinned in approval. "Hot."

"You are so weird," he whispered, bending to kiss my neck. I shivered at his touch, making the hairs on my arms stand up straight. "And so fucking mine." The shiver turned into a full-on quake, wreaking havoc through my body. "You like that, don't you?" he practically growled. "Being called mine."

I did, but still. "You cocky—"

His full lips covered mine, and I moaned as he dipped his tongue inside. The slick glide of his tongue against mine was something I'd never get enough of. He pulled back enough to whisper against my lips, "You taste so fucking sweet." Another kiss followed, a simple brush of his lips on mine. "I'm yours too, you know."

Memphis didn't give me time to respond before he took my mouth again, spinning me around and pushing me against the door. An inferno blazed through my body as he pressed flush against me, letting me feel every inch of what he claimed belonged to me. *Memphis was mine.* Damn right he was, and that meant I could do whatever I wanted. With my back pressed against the wall, it was a little hard to wiggle free, and for once, I was glad about my smaller size. I dropped to my knees, and Memphis's gaze burned hot as he stared down at me, watching silently as I lifted the hem of his hoodie and worked free the button and zipper of his jeans. The teeth parting whirred in the quiet room, heavy with Memphis's raspy breaths. "Tristan?"

I gripped the top of his jeans and boxer briefs, lowering them just enough that his hard cock sprang free, damn near slapping me in the face. Memphis's jaw ticced, and his hooded eyes filled with the heat of a blazing fire. "Suck it, babe. Let me see those perfect lips wrapped around my cock."

Gladly. Swiping my tongue over his tip, I moaned as the salty bead of pre-come burst in my mouth for the first time. He tasted better than I'd imagined. Better than anything had before. Memphis was my new favorite flavor, and I wanted more, demanded it, sucking him deep. There was nothing gentle about the way I bobbed my head along his cock. I worked him hard and fast, tightening my lips to the sound of his whispered words, murmuring how good it felt and promising he'd fuck me hard tonight.

I wanted him inside me again—bad. His filthy words

only spurred me on, causing my dick to throb in my tight jeans. I brought one hand to my fly, flicking it open, and pulled out my dick. I jerked myself hard at the same pace I fucked him with my mouth. Memphis wove his fingers through my hair, gripping tight as he held me in place, and then he began thrusting, forcing his cock to the back of my throat. I relaxed the muscles, letting him take as much as he needed, and let go of my dick to dig my fingers into his muscular thighs. I peered up at Memphis as he mumbled raspy curses while he set the pace, and stared down at his cock sliding between my lips.

Humming, I tongued the underside of his tip, loving the wild look that lit up his blue eyes. His jaw suddenly went slack, and he let out a long groan as he came, shuddering, and I greedily lapped up every salty drop. *Fuck*. Even without jerking off, my sac drew taut from the sounds he made. I needed to come and ripped my mouth away, focusing on my own orgasm as I wrapped my fingers tight around my shaft, stroking my dick while staring at him.

"Fuck, that's hot. Get up." Memphis didn't give me time to move. Softening dick still out, he reached under my arms, jerking me to my feet, then he dropped to his knees. "I've wanted your dick in my mouth again so fucking bad."

Memphis gripped the base of my cock, jerking me as he flicked my piercing with his tongue before covering my tip in the wet, warm cavern of his mouth. He sucked me to the back of his throat, working me in a rhythm that had a shout bursting from my lips in less than thirty seconds. He reached up, quickly slapping his palm over my mouth to cover the sound as an endless stream of come shot from my dick into his willing mouth. He greedily swallowed it, staring up at me with a gaze that consumed me in fire, causing a second wave of ecstasy to roll through me, slow and mellow, feeding him more. When I was spent, I sagged against the wall.

He rose, tucking his cock away, then took care of mine, but not without giving it one last leisurely stroke.

"Memphis," I sighed. I was a puddle of mush. There was no way I was up for anymore.

He zipped my jeans and leaned into me, brushing his full lips over mine, followed by a stinging nip to my lower lip. "I just wanted one last feel of what belongs to me."

"You're a horny bastard, you know that, right?" I grinned.

"I have to be if I want to keep my sex-crazed boyfriend happy." He smirked.

There was that word again, and it brought a dopey smile to my face that Memphis mirrored.

"I told my parents about you," I muttered, groggy.

"You did?" Memphis stilled, causing me to tense a bit. When an unexpected smile replaced his frozen expression, I relaxed. "I just didn't realize you'd be all-in like that," he explained. "What did they say?"

Shrugging, I sighed when he brushed my hair away from my sweaty forehead. "I met a firing squad of questions, but basically, they were cool about it. They wanted to come out to visit Saturday, but I know you have a game, so I'll be busy."

"You're actually going to come?" He tucked my hair behind one ear, which I hated because it totally messed up my look. But I wasn't going to tell him that when he was looking at me with that soft gaze.

"It's part of my new job description, isn't it?" I echoed his answer from earlier.

"Smartass." He pecked another kiss on my lips.

I chased after his lips when he pulled away until he chuckled. I pouted. "Ass. They also want to meet you."

Memphis froze again for a split second before clearing his throat. "Okay."

Noting the uneasy flash that had crossed his face, I assured him, "We don't have to do it right away or anything. I can tell them no."

Our relationship was so new, and neither of us really knew what we were doing, so I understood his hesitation. The situation was further complicated because I wasn't sure how and when Memphis planned on telling people, even if he had dragged me into a building in front of everyone. Actually, he'd manhandled me in public a few times now. I didn't want to question Memphis about where he stood on the subject. It would only add pressure on him mid-season when football alone offered him more than a heavy dose.

Memphis shook his head slightly. "No, it's fine."

"You sure?" I asked skeptically, studying his reaction.

"I'm sure." Memphis smiled, and I believed him. "I need to get going, so I'm not late to another practice. But I'll see you tonight. My place."

"I'll be there." Leaning into his touch, I practically purred, and he chuckled.

"Good." He popped the door open, and I frowned when he glanced out, scanning the hall. Of course, it made sense. It wouldn't matter if he had a girl in here. He'd do the same thing, but paranoia was a hard thing to kick. I wouldn't force Memphis to come out, but I didn't like the idea of being hidden either. If Memphis ever acted ashamed of me... I shook my head to clear the thought away, then pasted a smile on my face when he turned to face me, gesturing for me to follow. "All clear."

We stepped into the empty hallway, and I jerked to a

stop before turning and grabbed my milkshake, rescuing it from being abandoned.

Memphis shook his head as he eyed the drink. "Remind me to bring you more of those. Actually, no need. Pretty sure I'm going to remember that all on my own."

A wicked smile slanted his lips. Putty. I was putty in the fucker's hands. I reminded him, "You better get going."

"See you tonight." One more kiss, and I was staring at the back of my massive quarterback as he strode out of the building.

I wasn't sure if I loved Memphis, but I was positive I had it bad for him. It didn't occur to me until I was walking across campus to my next class that while I had admitted to telling my parents about us, Memphis hadn't uttered a word about telling his. Had he already? Did he even plan to?

I did my best to shut down the worrisome thoughts that were no doubt unnecessary anyway. Memphis would tell them.

SIXTEEN

MEMPHIS

TRISTAN HAD TOLD his parents about me, I thought as I secured my shoulder pads in place. It was almost impossible to think while surrounded by my rowdy teammates getting ready to take the field. Tonight was a big game, one that could very well make or break our chances of making the playoffs, but I found myself distracted. I hadn't thought much about telling my parents because I'd been so wrapped up in Tristan every free minute over the last several days.

He was insatiable in bed, not that I was complaining. Each morning when I'd woken with him in my arms, it had taken everything in me to part ways when we both had to get ready. It was unavoidable since I had practice, and he had class, otherwise I could have easily lain there all day. This morning we'd been able to sleep in a little later, and I'd soaked up the time with him, putting it to good use as I lazily pumped into his tight little body. I held back the groan that was itching to crawl up my throat, remembering what he'd looked like beneath me this morning. Tristan on his back, hard cock leaking onto his stomach, legs draped over my shoulders while I slowly slid in and out of his ass.

A burst of laughter behind me shook me from the sala-
cious memory and brought me back to the game. The game
my parents would be attending. The game where both my
parents and Tristan would be waiting outside the stadium
for me when it was over. *Fuck.* I hadn't told them about
Tristan yet. When he'd told me he'd let his parents in on our
relationship, I'd sort of panicked and blanked on responding
about mine. I planned to tell them. I swear I did. But again,
I was wrapped up in Tristan and honestly maybe a little
unsure. Not about Tristan. My feelings for him only deepened by day and took hold in a firmer grip by night.

I cursed under my breath as a pair of shoulder pads
knocked into mine, making me look over at Logan, who
stood next to me with concern. "You all right over
there, QB?"

I blew out a ragged breath. "Yeah, just have some shit on
my mind."

A vee formed between his eyebrows. "You better clear it
fast. We'll be heading out in less than ten minutes. We can't
win this game without you."

"I know, and I'm trying. I just got myself into a situation,
and I'm sort of dreading seeing my parents," I hedged as I
squeezed my jersey over my pads. "It's about Tristan."

Fully dressed, I propped my shoulder against the locker
toward Logan and scrubbed my hand over my shaven jaw.

"All right. Out with it." He mirrored my position. "Get it
off your chest before you go out there and play like shit. It's
not going to affect me because, after college, I'm done. But
you and some of the other guys on the team are counting on
the win for the future."

He was right, but the words stuck in my throat. If I
couldn't tell Logan, who was in a relationship with Colton,
how could I tell my parents? The guys around us were

fucking around, hyped for the game and not paying us any attention. I was out of time, so it was now or never. "I've been seeing him for a while."

Logan paused before a soft chuckle slid from his throat. "I knew you two were fucking. I swear I tried to believe you, but no one hangs out that much unless they are banging. How did I not realize you were gay?"

"Because I don't advertise it? I'm bi technically, but Tristan... I've never felt about anyone else the way I do about him," I admitted. "And we aren't just fucking, man. It's... more."

He knocked his fist into my shoulder, making it swing back. "Fucking a dude *and* fell in love with him."

"Love..." I shook my head, but the truth hit me like a tsunami. "Dude, seriously? Did you really have to say that shit right now?"

Logan cocked a brow. "You just now figuring it out?"

"I don't know. Maybe?" When had I fallen in love with Tristan? I couldn't pinpoint an exact moment. When I'd found him broken in need of someone to talk to, my heart had squeezed. When I saw him on campus for the first time, it had damn near beat out of my chest. When he confronted me on the porch at that party, calling me all those crazy-ass names that made absolutely no sense, I knew I had to be close to him. The first time we'd really kissed, I'd wanted to crawl my way inside of him like no one before. It had never been just about sex with Tristan. Did that mean I'd been falling the whole time? "You dick." I scowled at Logan. As if I didn't have enough on my mind, a crashing sense of worry thrashed around my chest. What if Tristan didn't feel the same way? I asked Logan as much.

Logan smirked. "I'm pretty sure that little dude is hard

up for you by the way he stares at you. Almost as much as you stare at him."

"Stare at him?" My brow furrowed because I had been sneaky as shit about it, hadn't I?

Logan chuckled. "Like I said, I *tried* to believe you when you said you two were just friends. But yeah, it was a hard sell."

Coach's voice cut through the sounds echoing in the locker room, and I knew he was getting ready to make his pregame speech. *Shit.*

"Okay, fine. What should I do?" I asked, needing quick advice. "All three of them will be waiting outside, and I haven't told my parents about him yet. They don't even know about me."

"Wow." His eyes widened. "You really are stupid."

"Logan," I warned.

Unfazed, he stared me dead in the eye. "Listen, right now, you clear your mind and get your fucking head in the game. You can't do anything to fix the situation until 'the game's over anyway. Worrying about stuff that could go wrong only puts you through it twice. If it goes south, it goes south."

"That is not helpful." I scowled.

"But it's the truth." Logan shrugged. "The thing is, even if it does blow up in your face, there's a thing called groveling. Let's hope it doesn't come to that, and you can explain it first, yeah?"

I glanced around the room at my teammates. Logan was right. These guys were counting on me to have my shit together. With determination and extreme hope I could make things right after the game, I grabbed my helmet and joined the circle forming around our head coach. Dropping to one knee, I focused on the positive energy swelling in the room with each word of encouragement and praise he spoke. We had this shit. When I hit the tunnel behind my team, I was ready. My jaw set and eyes focused. Coach ran out first onto the field with the rest of us jogging behind him.

The crowd's noise hit me first, followed by the cool breeze over my exposed skin and the smell of the turf. I lived and breathed the game. And now... My gaze swung to the student section, searching for a small bundle of all black. Tristan sat among the crowd, sticking out like a Gothic thumb. He waved and pointed at his shirt, causing a grin to split my lips when I saw my number printed in gold. He was wearing my jersey, or close enough, and now I wanted to see him wearing nothing *but* my jersey.

Now is not the time, Hale.

"Move it." Logan shoved me. "This is exactly what I'm talking about with the whole staring thing. Hard sell, dude. The worst."

Everyone would know soon anyway, so I let my gaze linger a second longer before I winked and turned away, chasing the adrenaline rush that flooded my system before each game.

———

THE GAME WAS everything it had been hyped to be. The Spartans had a solid defense, and I'd taken a few sacks. But their offense had been off their game just enough that we'd won by two touchdowns and an extra point.

My body was exhausted, but my nerves sizzled with anxious energy as I headed toward the exit. I swallowed hard and pushed through the door into the crowd of families waiting on their players. I spotted my mom and dad first under the bright lights that lit up the shadowed parking lot. Or rather, they spotted me and headed straight over. I shot them a tight grin as I scanned the swarm of people, looking for Tristan. I found him leaning against the wall messing with his phone. He glanced up, eyes meeting mine before he smiled and pushed off the wall.

I had this weird moment of panic where three people walked toward me—two of them had no idea the third even existed. It was then I realized I wouldn't be able to fix it. The collision was coming, and I had no idea what the wreckage would look like once it was over.

"Memphis, oh my god, honey! What a great game!" my mom crowed as she swooped in for a hug while I reluctantly met my dad for a high-five over her head. Of course, this couldn't be a game they'd miss. All the while, I watched Tristan come to a stop several feet away as he watched on, seemingly unsure of his place.

"Mom. Dad." I cleared my throat. "I have—"

My mom interrupted me, "We're taking you out to eat to celebrate. Your dad made reservations at Pablo's, so I hope that's okay. We hate to rush, but we have a last-minute flight to San Diego in a few hours."

"San Diego?" I questioned.

Dad pulled my mom away, and she rolled her eyes. He explained, "We are trying to secure a deal to buy a few commercial properties in our area. The guy doesn't want to make the back-and-forth trips anymore, and we don't want to pass up the opportunity."

Speaking of opportunities, I looked at Tristan again, and my parents followed my gaze.

"Do you know him?" Mom asked.

I waved him over. Tristan scanned over my parents before closing the distance.

"This is Tristan. Tristan, my parents, Veronica and Warren," I introduced them.

"Nice to finally meet you," Tristan said, creeping closer to my side. He was nervous, I realized, and felt like shit all over again.

"Oh, nice to finally meet you, too?" My mom sounded confused. Of course, she did. She was likely focused on the *finally* part. "How do you two know each other?"

Her gaze flicked from me to Tristan and back again, with a slight crease formed on her surgically enhanced forehead. I quickly glanced at my father, who appeared bored, probably ready to talk about the game.

"Um..." Tristan looked to me for help, likely just realizing I hadn't told them about our relationship. Damn it.

"Tristan is..." All eyes swung toward me... and I froze. I fucking froze.

Every single one of them stared at me expectantly, growing more awkward the longer the words stuck in my throat. Hurt clouded Tristan's ice-blue eyes, and he stepped back.

"We're just friends," he told my parents, and it felt like a dagger through my gut. He wasn't finished. "Sorry, Mr. and Mrs. Hale, it was nice to meet you, but I just remembered I need to check on my cat. Pretty sure she has rabies."

I blinked. Tristan didn't even have a cat, and the excuse was seriously lame. I was pretty sure it was intended for shock factor. It worked.

"Tristan—" I started at the same time my mom gasped. "Oh, well I... I'm sorry. I hope she's okay."

He hummed. "She'll be fine, I'm sure. I just need to take her to a hypnotist and probably an acupuncturist."

Jesus. He was really on a roll. My parents appeared flat-out baffled, eyeing him as if he were insane, which was arguably a good assumption after that word vomit he'd just spewed. And it was my fucking fault.

Without another word, he turned on his heels and left me standing there watching him walk out of my life. And I knew that's exactly what he was doing.

Fuck. *Fuck.*

"What was that about?" my mom hissed. "Rabies?"

"That was odd," my dad agreed, and I couldn't exactly argue with him.

Shaking my head, I stepped back. "I just royally fucked up."

My dad gave me a quizzical frown and glanced to where Tristan was quickly gaining distance. "Explain."

"That. Him..." I gestured toward Tristan while already moving backward. "My boyfriend is walking away because I fucked up."

My parents both stood still with wide eyes. "Boyfriend?"

Dad squared his shoulders. "If this is some joke—"

"It's not. And I'm sorry to spring this on both of you like this, but I'm more concerned about how he must feel right now. I'll tell you everything later," I promised as I glanced back toward Tristan, gauging the distance as he started to blend in with the shadows.

"Soon, Memphis," my dad demanded. "You have a lot of explaining to do."

I did, but not because he was ordering it. I did because I owed it to myself. I did because I had every intention of mending things between Tristan and me, even if I had to beg.

With that, I ran off, following Tristan as he stalked across the parking lot toward his car.

"Tristan!" I yelled as I kicked up my speed until I was sprinting.

He glanced over his shoulder, rolling his eyes, but the hurt was still evident. I knew him. Knew Tristan would throw walls up around his emotions and freeze me out. I wasn't going to let that happen.

"Leave me alone, Memphis," he said and continued the trek to his car.

"Let me explain. I fucking froze, and I'm sorry." *Damn it.* He wouldn't even look at me.

"So am I," he ground out.

"Sorry?" I asked, baffled. What did Tristan have to apologize for? He'd done nothing wrong.

He didn't bother with a reply, simply pressed his key fob, the lights on his red car flashing as he approached. He popped open the door, ignoring me altogether.

"I told them," I explained as he lowered into the seat. I caught the door as he attempted to slam it closed, nearly catching my fingers in the process.

His head jerked up, and he glared.

"Too slow," I said as I jerked the door open wider.

Tristan narrowed his eyes further as he gritted out, "What do you want? I told you I'm in a hurry."

"Right." I nodded. "The cat that you don't have. Sounded serious."

"It is. Now, if you'll kindly remove your big ass, I'll be on my way."

"I'm afraid I can't do that." I propped my forearm above the door and leaned down, whispering, "I'm sorry."

"For what?" he asked casually.

I sighed. "Stop acting like you aren't mad at me."

He swallowed hard and shook his head. "I'm not mad. I'm...frustrated at myself. I knew better."

"Knew better than what?" Panic was starting to make

my heart thump wildly as I waited for his response. It seemed to take forever as he stared right through me.

"To date a straight guy," he finally whispered.

What the fuck? "I'm not exactly straight, Tristan. And you know that."

"You know what I mean. Everyone thinks you are. Now, let go," he demanded with tears filling his eyes. My chest ached and my hold on the door loosened as the gravity of what I'd done hit me full force. Those seconds that I'd let him down had shattered him.

"Tristan, I'm so sorr—"

"Leave me alone." He took the opportunity to slam the door closed and revved the engine.

I knocked on the window. "Listen to me, damn it."

The sound of the gears shifting told me I was out of time, and I had to fix it now. I knocked harder, but he stared straight ahead. And then he was gone, leaving me standing there, staring at his tail lights. Was I supposed to give him time to cool down? Would he just make himself more miserable? I had no idea if I'd make the situation worse, but I *had* to go after him. He had to know everything. I turned to hurry to my truck and found my parents standing right behind me. How much had they seen or heard?

"We need to talk," I rasped out. This conversation was long overdue, and my parents couldn't have seen this coming before tonight. I understood why they appeared so confused.

"Maybe we should take this somewhere else." My mom glanced around for prying ears. They were everywhere, and many had to have witnessed me getting shut the fuck down by a guy.

"I don't have time for that." With a deep sigh and running my fingers through my hair, I began, "Tristan and I are dating. He's my boyfriend. I'm bi." At my parents' puzzled expressions, I clarified, "Bisexual."

"What?"

"That isn't true. You've never shown any signs..." They talked over each other, and my dad looked like a stroke was imminent.

"Stop it," I raised my voice. "Why would I make that up?"

My mom's eyes filled with worry. "You are going to ruin everything you've worked so hard for—"

"Hang on. I haven't killed anybody or burned anything down. Or God forbid, quit football." I grew more frustrated with each word as I unloaded everything I'd been holding back for years. "This is why I never told y'all. I really am more than just a guy who can throw a football. This is who I am and who I've always been. Take it or leave it. This is your son."

After a lengthy pause, my dad shook his head and was the first to break the stare-off. "That guy? Just you being... bisexual"—he cleared his throat—"is going to be hard enough for the public to accept."

I felt my face and voice tighten in steely determination and anger. "His name is Tristan Stafford, and he is perfect for me. Eccentric, yes. But in the best way. He makes me happy. And I'm sorry but I couldn't give two fucks about what you, the *public*, or anyone else, thinks of me or our relationship."

Silence ticked by for a minute before my mother added her thoughts. "He didn't seem interested in hearing you out. Honey, maybe that's for the best. Going into the NFL—"

They weren't listening, and my temper grew. "Plenty of players are out now, Mom." My gaze slid to meet my father's. "I knew you both wouldn't approve. But this is me, okay? You can either accept me or not. But it won't change who I am. I don't want it to. I've never felt the way he makes me feel. Accepted. Wanted. For me. And not just a quarterback. So, you either accept him... me... us, or you lose me altogether."

My dad sighed and rubbed his temple. "Memphis, it's not that we wouldn't accept you. I will admit I wasn't prepared to hear it. You've never shown any signs."

Signs. He repeated the word as if they were symptoms.

"It's not an illness." I scowled.

My dad scowled back. "That's not what I meant. Don't try to put words in my mouth. Mostly I'm concerned for you, but it's not only your career I'm worried about. There will be challenges. Are you prepared for that?"

"Prepared, no. Ready? I've been ready for years. It's been ripping me apart inside." That admission seemed to impact them more than anything else I'd said as their expressions morphed to sadness. My parents cared about me, I knew that, but sometimes it felt like they only cared because of my ability to win. Hales won. That simple.

Mom stepped forward and rubbed her hand over my arm. "I'm sorry you felt like you couldn't tell us."

A sigh escaped my throat. "I knew you'd bring up the NFL, and I was afraid you'd try to talk me out of coming out. At that time, I might have let you. I didn't have anything driving me toward it, but I do now. Tristan means a lot to me. More than other people's opinions." I was repeating myself, but I wanted to make sure they understood. This was happening with or without their blessing.

Mom gripped my wrists. "And you're positive you want to do this?"

I gave a curt nod. "There's not a doubt in my mind."

She sighed, and my dad huffed. His roughened voice strained. "Then we will support you."

I hid my surprise. That hadn't been the response I'd expected. "And Tristan," I demanded.

"Don't be so dramatic, Memphis." My mom patted her hair as if making sure not a single strand was out of place. "We will support you both. It won't be easy on him if you get drafted."

"When, not if," my dad corrected, and my mom nodded.

"I have to go." I'd said my piece, and I had already taken too long to go after Tristan. But I wanted to be able to tell him I'd finally made the leap. We'd be out in public. Everyone would know I was in love with him. Even if he didn't forgive me, I would still tell everyone who'd listen.

"Then you better hurry," my dad said, surprising me. "Believe it or not, we do see you as more than a football player. Had I realized you'd thought otherwise... I wish I could go back and change that. All we can do is apologize and support you going forward. Now go before you lose that boy." He stared at me meaningfully.

If I hadn't already, I heard even though he hadn't voiced it. With a nod, I ran to my truck and hauled ass toward Tristan's apartment, hoping that was where he'd gone. When I pulled into the apartment complex, there was no sign of his red sports car in the lot. And when I knocked, no sounds came from the other side of the door.

Pulling my phone from my pocket, I texted him.

Me: *Where are you?*

I sank onto the hard concrete, leaning against the wall next to his door, waiting for a reply. After five minutes of no response, I tried again.

Me: *Hear me out, please. I told my parents everything. And I'm going to tell everyone else too.*

Still nothing. I texted Nash.

Me: *Has Rendon heard from Tristan?*

Nash: *Just asked him. He said no. What happened?*

Me: *I fucked up, but I'm trying to fix it.*

My phone rang, and Nash's voice came over the line, a bite lacing his tone. "What did you do?"

I explained everything, and Nash groaned. "You're an idiot."

"I know, okay?" I rubbed my eyes. "There's more."

I spilled the whole story. The night I'd met Tristan—leaving out the specifics of what he'd gone through because that wasn't my story to tell and why I'd avoided him—again being vague.

"What the fuck? You serious?" Nash understandably sounded confused.

"Very."

"Okay, well, this is fixable. Just hound the fuck out of him. Worked for me." Though the advice sounded disturbing, he wasn't wrong. Nash had been ruthless in his pursuit of Rendon, and it had worked. But Tristan and Rendon couldn't be more different. Tristan was unpredictable at best, so I had no idea what would happen. But I had to try.

Once I hung up, I waited for two hours, but Tristan never came home.

I SPENT the rest of the weekend at my parents' house, and though they kept asking what was wrong because they'd had plans to visit me and instead I'd come to them, I'd insisted I was fine. I wasn't. And when they'd asked me about Memphis, I'd lied and said he'd had plans.

My phone had blown up with fifteen missed calls and twenty-two texts from Memphis. I read all of them because I hadn't been able to stop myself. I wanted to respond. He'd told his parents. He planned to tell everyone. But what he'd done, or rather not done, had stung. The same guy who had convinced me to be strong and stand my ground, giving zero fucks about what people thought, had been the same guy who had frozen when it was time to introduce me as his boyfriend. All of those old insecurities had rushed to the surface and threatened to tear me down. Of all the people who tried to make me feel less than, I'd never expected Memphis to be among them. And for those few seconds, waiting for him to acknowledge what we were to his parents, I'd felt the stirring of shame. Not ashamed of myself, but what I imagined Memphis felt over our relationship. If I forgave him, moved on... how would it feel if he did it again? I'd be fucking crushed.

This is what I got for trying to date a closeted guy—a smashed heart. I knew better than to catch feelings for someone like Memphis. Except I didn't know anyone else like him, so it really wasn't my fault.

No, I wouldn't demand he tell the world he was into guys before he was ready. Still, I wouldn't pretend to be insignificant around other people either. He hadn't even warned me his parents would be at the game, so I hadn't been prepared to be dismissed as a friend. Well, that's who I'd told them I was because Memphis had grown pale.

I wanted to call Rendon and purge my misery, but I'd held back. Once Memphis had outted us as a couple to Nash, Rendon had called me the next day. I'd been a little *ahem* busy, so I'd just confirmed what he'd been told and proceeded to get tangled up in my boyfriend all over again. My gut twisted. *Ex-boyfriend.*

No, I couldn't talk to Rendon. He'd run to Nash. Nash would probably bitch at Memphis, and I didn't want that. I just wanted to mean as much to Memphis as he meant to me. Or at least I had before Saturday night.

Rabies. Shaking my head, I thought over what I'd told his mom and dad. Not one of my better stories, admittedly, but it held the intended impact based on everyone's shocked expressions.

As I crossed campus Monday morning to my history class, I was mulling over the last forty-eight hours. Lost in thought, I barely heard the footsteps pounding the sidewalk behind me and jumped when a hand gripped my arm.

I whirled around, knocking the hand away, only to find Memphis staring down at me. "Didn't you hear me calling you?"

Rolling my eyes, I turned and spoke over my shoulder, "No, and I don't want to talk now."

"Would you stop for a second? I've been losing my mind since Saturday night. Where were you? Did you read my texts?" He matched my steps, shooting the rapid-fire questions.

"Leave me alone, Memphis." I picked up my pace, but he only quickened his strides.

"Did you read them?" he repeated. "I told my parents like the second you drove away. I swear. I fucked up. I know that."

I spun on my heels, and he stopped on a dime. "You made me feel like shit, Memphis. You. Of all fucking people, I never thought you'd be the one who did that to me."

Memphis's expression grew sad as I gave voice to the emotions he'd stirred in me. He blew out a long breath. "I'm so sorry, Tristan. It wasn't about you. It was about me." He shoved his hands in his pockets, staring down at me with sincerity shining in his eyes, but I'd been there and knew what I'd heard and seen.

I huffed, swiping my hair from my forehead. "Yeah, okay."

"I'm serious, Tris. I wasn't prepared and froze." He shook his head.

I wanted to believe him. My traitorous heart demanded I hear him out, but I shut that bitch down. She'd created enough problems. "Yeah, well, nice talk. See you later."

When I began to walk away again, he trailed me. Shocker. Stubborn jock. "No, damn it. Tristan, you are every fucking thing to me. Let me prove it."

I scoffed. "How do you plan to do that?"

Memphis stopped walking, surprising me he'd given up

so easily. I glanced back and found Memphis squaring his shoulder, cupping his hand around his mouth. What the hell was he doing? I turned to watch because I couldn't help it.

"'Tristan Stafford is the best thing that has ever happened to me!" he shouted in that deep timbre that fucked with my head. "I'm so stupid in love with him, and he has no idea! He's my boyfriend, whether he likes it or not. And I'm going to do everything I can to prove it to him, starting with telling everyone. I love Tristan Stafford's crazy ass. He owns me. Does anyone have a problem with that?"

My cheeks lit with fire as I glanced around, taking in all of the stares from students who'd simply been walking by before he'd grabbed their attention. A repeat of the entire student body looking at me all over again. Except this time, it wasn't because someone had spread the message that I was gross. Memphis... "You love me?" I whispered.

Memphis shook his head. "You have no idea how bad I have it for you. I'm fucking crazy about you. I... "

"You what?" I prodded. "Say it again. To me this time."

Memphis stared straight into my eyes. With a soft shake of his head, a slow chuckle escaped his lips. "I'm stupid in love with you, Tris."

My witty comebacks died in my smart mouth. *Memphis loved me? "Why?"

Memphis barked a laugh. "Because you're smart. Funny. You make me smile and laugh more than I ever did before you came along. You healed a part of me that night, too, you know. I never stopped thinking about you, wondering if you were okay. I had to keep myself from tracking you down so many times." His fingers dug into my hips. "You make me happy. I just want to make you happy too."

"Oh." That had been a lot more than I'd expected. Like *a lot* more.

I chewed on my lip, mulling everything over. "Sooo, what is happening right now?"

"Right now, I'm waiting for my boyfriend to forgive me... and then hoping for some makeup sex." His dimple popped.

"You can't bribe me with sex, Memphis Hale." I scowled, not appreciating him going after my weak spot.

"Is it working?" He leaned in closer, almost nose to nose, bringing the scent of his warm body wash and minty breath. "I still want to try you fucking me."

"You are playing dirty." Smart and Sexy. Lethal fucker.

Sensing victory, Memphis quirked his lips. "Weren't you the one that told me you were as dirty as they *come*?"

"Not so you could use it against me later, rainbow donkey jerk," I snapped, and he sobered.

Memphis frowned. "I'm sorry, Tris. I don't want to pressure you. I just... Fuck, I don't want to lose you." Memphis's nostrils flared.

"Oh." That's all I had in response because I was still processing his words.

Memphis grinned, but it seemed uncertain. "Oh? That's it?"

I bit my lip as I stared into his deep blue eyes that were watching me so closely. "Your parents think I have a cat with rabies."

He blinked, long and slow. "Tristan, no one with half a brain believed that bullshit story."

"Yeah, it was a pretty bad one," I agreed.

Memphis grimaced. "You seriously just going to leave me hanging here?"

I sighed as the truth came tumbling out whether I

approved or not. "Fine. Memphis Hale, I loved you before I even knew it was you. When you kidnapped me—"

"I did *not* kidnap you," Memphis interrupted.

"Agree to disagree," I offered. "When you kidnapped me, I wasn't sure what I was getting myself into, but *this* was definitely not on my radar. I didn't know I would end up wanting to get matching tattoos."

"You don't have any tattoos, and I'm not getting any." Memphis immediately vetoed the idea, grinning as his whole body drained of tension. His relief was palpable, and just then, I realized the depth of his worry.

I'd meet him in the middle. "Just a small one."

"Nope." He shook his head.

"We'll see," I decided.

"No, we won't," Memphis argued, but it was still on the table as far as I was concerned. "Tristan, I'm not getting a tattoo."

I grinned.

"Shit. I'm getting a fucking tattoo, aren't I?" Memphis asked while squeezing his eyes closed.

"Just a small one," I promised.

His eyes opened slowly, and he sighed. "I love you, even if you're seriously weird."

"I love you back, even if you have to be a jock." Reaching up to the giant football player, I circled his neck and pulled him down toward me. Pressing my lips to his, I didn't give a fuck who was watching anymore. Memphis groaned, slipping his tongue into my mouth. I sucked on it, and his fingers dug into my ass as he pulled back, mumbling against my lips, "Does this mean you forgive me?"

"Duh." I snorted, grinning as our breaths laced together. He puffed out a relieved breath and then laughed as I pulled him toward me for more tongue action.

With his hands on my hips, he pulled back the slightest bit, chuckling when I fought not to release him. "As much as I never want to let you out of my sight ever again, I'm already late. I'll come over tonight. Be home."

Right. Because there wasn't a chance I was going anywhere now anyway. "Where are you going?" I asked when he stood to his full height, stretching out his back.

"Practice. I'm already going to catch so much shit, but I had to find you first." He took a step back, reminding me, "Be home."

"Uh-huh," I mumbled as he grinned and turned, jogging toward the athletic complex.

Staring after him, I ignored everyone around me and dug my phone from my pocket, calling Rendon. He picked up on the third ring. "What's up?"

"Memphis loves me," I blurted as it really sank in how much he cared about me.

"Tristan, did he actually say that, or are you just being *you*?" Rendon sighed.

I scowled at the phone. "No, ass. He just told me."

"Seriously?" He sounded surprised, even when in the background, Nash quickly followed with, "I fucking knew it."

"Are you two ever not together?" I rolled my eyes.

"Unfortunately, because of his schedule, we're apart more often than I like." Rendon didn't sound happy about that fact at all but quickly shifted topics. "Back to Memphis. Did you say it back? How did this happen? Y'all only started dating like a few days ago." He was understandably baffled

"Actually, it's a long story. It started about a year and a half ago when he kissed me," I explained.

"What?" Rendon asked at the same time as Nash said, "Yeah, he mentioned that."

Memphis had been serious. Apparently, he was going to tell everyone and had even gotten an early start, but apparently Nash had once again withheld information Rendon would be pissed about, which made sense because Rendon hadn't mentioned anything to me. I was met with silence once I told Rendon the full story.

"What the fuck?" Rendon breathed out, uncharacteristically cursing.

"Yeah," I agreed, because the story had to come as a surprise. "But that's our twisted fairytale." He only repeated the curse. Apparently, I'd shocked my best friend to the point of only being capable of those three words. "So... advice on dating a pro baller? I think I'm going to need it eventually."

MY KNEES RUBBED on the couch as I squirmed, bent over while Memphis ran his tongue over my asshole. He'd been putting his talented mouth to work on my dick and ass for the last fifteen minutes, and I couldn't take it anymore, especially after waiting all day after his confession to see him again. My legs shook as I rested my head on my folded arms over the back on the couch, moving my hips, seeking more.

"Stop teasing me," I panted.

"You want my cock, baby?" Memphis growled and squeezed my ass. "You want me here?" He rubbed the pad of his thumb over my spit-slicked hole. "Want me to show you how bad I want you? How crazy you make me?"

"Fuck yes." I moaned as he slipped his thumb inside my overly sensitive rim. "Now."

He pulled back, chuckling as I heard the sound of

ripping foil and the lube cap snap open. "You are absolutely perfect. You know that, right?"

I glanced over my shoulder, feeling his tip press against my asshole. "Show me."

His eyelids drooped, lust and love shining from the deep blue orbs. "I love you," he rasped, and then he pressed forward, making my eyes roll back. "I want you. That's never going to change."

"Don't stop now," I begged when he was balls deep. "You can fuck me slow later. My dick is so hard, it hurts."

"Okay, baby. I'll give you what you want. But later, I'm taking my time," he promised on a groan as he pulled back. "I want to live buried inside of you."

I shook my head. "Later, you're going to feel my dick inside of you."

Memphis growled, slamming back in hard, ripping a moan from my throat. "Fuck yes. Make those sounds for me, baby," he demanded, sounding as gone as I felt. "You want to fuck me, don't you?"

"Yes. But right now, I need you to make me come." I was not beyond begging and pushed back, encouraging him to pick up the pace.

"Yes, sir." He moved inside me like it was his sole mission to drain every ounce of pleasure from my body while filling me with whispered words of how much he loved me and how amazing my ass felt around his cock.

I'd never get tired of hearing how he felt about me. How bad he wanted to fuck me came in a close second. I'd never get enough of the feel of him stretching me wide. It was different having sex with someone I loved, knowing Memphis loved me back. I was filled in a new way, one that saturated my heart and soul along with my body.

"I'm close," I warned, and he fucked me harder, reaching

around me to grab my dick, jerking me in time with his thrusts. I came hard with his name on my lips, and he followed, emptying his balls inside of me, slowly pumping until we both sagged on the cushions.

Memphis caught his breath first, partially because I'd been squashed beneath him, and then pressed his lips to my neck. "Let's shower. I want to lie down with you."

"And hold me close? You sappy shit." I grinned.

"Shut up. I almost lost you. I need to hold you, okay?" He laughed and tugged me to my feet.

I stopped him, pulling him down to kiss him, and nipped his lip. "I love you. I'm not going anywhere."

Memphis let out a stuttered breath. "Good. Because honestly, I'm not sure how I'd handle it."

"Well, you don't have to worry about it. I'm yours," I assured him.

"I meant it when I said you owned me, Tristan." He pressed another kiss to my lips. "Now come on."

I let him drag me down the hall to the bathroom, where he cranked on the shower and proceeded to clean me up, worshipping my body with his hands, caressing and touching every inch of me. When Memphis stared at me the way he was now, as if I was his entire world, I felt whole. Memphis completed me when I hadn't realized a part of me was missing until he filled the empty space. I didn't know how our future would play out, but later, when he was wrapped around me, crushing my lungs, I knew one thing for sure. I was investing in a body pillow.

EPILOGUE

MEMPHIS/THREE YEARS LATER

WITH HER HAIR tied up in a gray-laced bun, Tristan's mom was busy at the counter chopping red peppers to add to a pasta dish. I stepped around her petite frame to grab silverware from a drawer to add to the table settings.

Some Christmas movie was playing on the TV in the living room, but no one watched it. However, in the worst off-key tone I could imagine, Tristan was singing along as he stirred a pot of creamy white sauce on the stove.

"Memphis, hun, would you mind taking this to the table?" Mrs. Stafford nodded her head toward a wicker basket that held fresh buttery garlic bread.

The meal was odd and definitely atypical of a traditional Christmas dinner, but it had been the same every year. A Stafford tradition I had gotten behind the first Christmas Tristan and I had spent with his parents. Now that I'd been drafted to the Florida Panthers, my diet had kicked up to a new level of strict—much to Tristan's horror—so food like this was a once-a-year indulgence.

"Yes, ma'am." I added the basket to my haul, taking it all to the separate dining room with an old-fashioned wood table centered in the room. Adorned with a red tablecloth trimmed in green ribbon, the table setting matched the colorful festive decor that Mrs. Hale had filled their older two-story home with, from top to bottom. Ropes of garland with bright pops of holly were woven around the staircase banister, and topped the mantel over a cozy fire burning in the large brick fireplace. In the corner of the living room, a seven-foot Christmas tree stood tall, decked out in colorful lights, with shiny red tinsel draped on the faux-snow-covered branches.

The ambiance was a stark contrast to the modern white-on-white color scheme my parents preferred. Still, I always enjoyed Christmas with the Staffords more than I did when we made the trip to my parents' small holiday celebration.

As I set down the garlic bread then laid out the forks and knives beside the Christmas plates, which were embellished with a painted wreath in the center, heat seeped through the back of my shirt. Tristan pressed in against me, bringing a hint of cinnamon to my nose.

"You look kinda hot all domesticated and shit." He snickered when I shot him a look over my shoulder.

"And what about you?" I turned and gestured to the weird as hell purple apron he was wearing covered in splatters of sauce.

Tristan glanced down at the apron. "I'm wearing all black. I'm not messing up my clothes."

"I didn't know you could cook anyway." I cocked a brow, smirking down at him. "You've been holding out on me, letting me do all the heavy lifting."

Tristan grinned because he'd been getting away with that secret for years now. "And you'll forget you witnessed anything the minute we leave here. My mom makes me help out, but I'm too used to you spoiling me to keep this up at home."

Home was a condo in Florida the team had initially set up for us until I had been offered my four-year contract. Now that my first season was coming to a close, I felt comfortable in my position with the Panthers and planned to invest in something much more our style than the uppity building we resided in on the twenty-third floor.

"Nope." I tugged him until he was flush with my chest, and he glanced up, pale blue eyes twinkling with humor. "It will be good for us. Couple activities and all."

"Forget it, Hale." Tristan traced a finger in a circle over my nipple, and I snatched his hand, bringing it to my mouth to nip his finger. "But I'll happily contribute to dessert."

I sucked on his fingertip. "You aren't talking about food, are you?"

"Do you want me to be talking about food?" The mischievous smile perking up his lips said he knew the answer already.

Slowly, I shook my head. "Not even close."

"Good, because I—"

"Tristan, the sauce is going to curdle if you don't get back in here!" Mrs. Stafford called out.

Tristan sighed as he stepped back. "That's me. Tristan, sauce-stirrer extraordinaire."

I swatted his ass as he turned and headed for the kitchen. The side door opened with a thud, and Mr. Stafford, a tall, slim man with black hair and blue eyes, entered the house, lugging an assortment of wrapped gifts. He glanced at me, explaining, "Can't set them out early. Cat."

He didn't need to explain further. My aunt had a kitten one Christmas when we had stayed the night. That morning we didn't need to bother unwrapping anything. "Do you need help?"

"If you wouldn't mind. There's more in the garage." He tipped his head toward the open door.

As I stepped into the garage, my heart raced as I thought about Tristan's gift sitting in my pocket, feeling twenty times heavier than it should. With all of the rubbing on me Tristan couldn't seem to stop himself from doing, I was surprised he hadn't noticed the square bulge and questioned what was in there. I was more nervous than I'd been during my first professional football game, and I still had to get through dinner before I could hopefully breathe easier.

After helping arrange the gifts around the tree, I was relieved when Mrs. Stafford finally told us dinner was ready. As we sat around the table, the conversation shifted to the topics of extended family I had yet to meet and asking me questions about my season with the Florida Panthers. While asking Tristan question after question about how his online counseling gig was going—amazingly well for a newly formed practice—all I could think about was what I had planned once the table was cleared.

The time came what felt like an eternity later and the blink of an eye all at once. With Mr. Stafford lazily lounging on the living room recliner and Mrs. Stafford packing away leftovers, I grabbed Tristan's hand where we sat on the couch. "Want to go for a walk?"

His eyebrows dipped. "When have I ever voluntarily participated in exercise?"

Never, I thought with a grin. "Come on. I'm not used to eating such heavy food. I need to get moving and want you to go with me."

He sighed with exasperation. "It's a good thing I love you, Hale, or this would be a deal-breaker."

I stood and pulled him to his feet.

"We'll be back," Tristan told his parents while sighing dramatically. "We're going for a walk, apparently."

When Tristan headed for the door, I looked at his dad, who mouthed *good luck,* and then at his mom, who had her hand pressed to her chest as she wiped under her eyes with the other. They knew what I was about to do. Only Tristan was in the dark. It had taken a while for them to stop worrying I'd break Tristan's heart, but when they realized I loved their son more than I could ever explain, they'd welcomed me with open arms.

"You coming or what?" Tristan stood next to the coat rack, tugging on his jacket before he tossed me my hoodie. "This was your brilliant idea."

I hoped it was brilliant. "I'm coming."

"That's what he said," he murmured, because it was Tristan.

I bit my lip, studying my insane boyfriend, trying to imagine him wearing a ring that promised he'd be mine forever. Fuck, why was I so nervous?

We headed out into the cold night, taking the steps out onto the sidewalk in the quiet neighborhood.

As we strolled along the pavement, Tristan nudged my side. "Are you okay? You haven't said a word since we left the house."

Not out loud, I thought. I'd been busy running over my speech for the hundredth time. "Yeah. Just thinking."

"About?" he prodded.

I tipped my head as I nodded to the familiar tree that still stood tall. "That's where we met."

Tristan glanced at the yard, specifically at the tree we'd sat under that night. "It is. What if I'd landed in a different yard?" he wondered aloud. "We might not have met."

I shook my head. "I think you're wrong. I would have noticed you on campus anyway."

"Maybe," he agreed. "You might not have ignored me, and things could have played out differently. We might not have been here right now."

He was right. "See? I knew what I was doing from the start."

Tristan snorted. "Liar. You would have ignored me forever if I hadn't confronted you for being an *egotistical asshole*. Sorry about that, by the way."

"I'm not." Remembering that night on the porch and the fire in his eyes as he'd berated me over my lack of acknowledgment brought a smile to my lips. "It wasn't even close to the weirdest thing you've called me. But Evil Chicken Nugget was the first."

Tristan laughed quietly. "Now, you're just my sexy strawberry milkshake."

"Fuck, you're weird," I said on a chuckle. "At least I'm no longer a jock hippo on your phone."

Tristan snorted. He'd been pissy as hell when I'd found the stupid name and changed it, but that was probably more to do with the fact that I'd replaced it with *Spank Bank Material*.

The laughter caught in my throat as we circled the block, nearing the spot I'd first kissed him.

Tristan turned toward me with a raised brow when I slowed to a stop and tugged on his hand. "What are you doing?"

I took a deep breath and sank down on one knee. His brow furrowed in question as I reached into my pocket. His jaw dropped when I pulled out the black velvet box, then reached out to take his shaking hand. "Something I'm hoping you'll say yes to."

"Yes," he said immediately, and I barked a laugh, all the nerves vanishing with knowing his answer already. I loved him so much. More than I knew I had been capable of. Tristan owned every part of me. Good and bad. I wasn't perfect, and neither was he, but we were perfect together, and I wanted it to last for the rest of our lives.

"Not yet. I have things to say, if you don't mind, of course." I grinned

He nodded slowly, gaze intent on mine. "Proceed. Quickly please."

"Tristan," I began and cleared my throat. "You are my hurricane, a colorful whirl of insults that make no sense, and a huge heart you never could hide even when you wanted to. I saw it. I saw you. You bring out the best in me, offer me the kind of love I never knew I could give or receive. You are my world. I'd give anything and everything I have to keep you by my side for the rest of my life."

"What else?" he pressed.

I chewed on my lip. "Um, that's sort of it. I—"

"Good. Can I please see it now?" He wiggled greedy fingers.

Shit. I knew I'd fuck it up. I popped open the box, revealing the solid onyx band. "Will you marry me?"

"I said yes already," he pointed out, a wide smile splitting his lips.

"Say it again," I whispered.

The wide smile melted into a softer one as his eyes focused on me kneeling at his feet. "Yes, Memphis. I only want to be yours. Now and forever."

A rush of gratitude for the smart-mouthed man who'd unexpectedly entered my life so many years ago flowed through my body. I slid the ring on to his finger, and he quickly examined it before attempting to pull me to my feet, something he'd never manage. I stood and bent down, kissing him and pouring all my love for him into the touch.

"I love you," he mumbled against my lips.

Those words always created the same reaction in me. They lit my heart on fire. "I love you too."

We'd come full circle. From the night my life had changed forever, when a colorful hurricane stirred up my world, to now, the beginning of our forever.

The End

ACKNOWLEDGMENTS

This book wouldn't have been published without my incredibly appreciated support team.

Kid one and two, you better never actually be reading this. You two rock for understanding and finding ways to keep busy while I was stationed in front of my laptop for hours on end.

To my loudest cheerleader, my mom, you are probably the biggest reason my books see the light of day. Thank you for all your pep talks and all-around support.

Huge shout-out to Reese Knightley and Rheland Richmond for keeping me motivated and on track while writing Memphis and Tristan's story.

Jamie Piatt, I'm so glad you've joined my team. You are an absolute rock star.

Kathy, you know I couldn't do this without you.

My Crow's Clubhouse reader group, you all are amazing. It's nice to know I've got my own corner of the online world filled with readers and authors who support my work and provide a positive and fun atmosphere.

Thank you to the many authors, groups and blogs that help spread the word of Delayed Game.

To you, the reader, I couldn't do this whole author thing without you. Thank you for reading, reviewing, recommending and sharing the book. It means the absolute world to me.

XOXO -Baylin

ABOUT BAYLIN

Bios are challenging. I don't have a clue how to write about myself. Fictional characters? Sure! Me? Not so much. It's the reason my author bio stayed practically blank until after I finished my second novel.

Who am I? Well, I guess I should start by telling you that I write MM romance and I love what I do.

I fell in love with writing during elementary school with my first "Bare Book" but honestly never thought I'd become an author. It always seemed to be something I dreamed of and not something I could make a reality. Now that I have, I can't picture myself doing anything else.

I live in Texas where the heat and I don't get along. One day I hope to call Northeast USA home. I'm a mother of two ridiculously cute kids and a "grandmother" to Lilah, the sweetest cat in the world. When she wants to be.

Spending the day under a fluffy blanket reading or writing away on my laptop with a mountain of coffee is my idea of time well spent. I get to live so many lives through books that I consider myself genuinely lucky to call myself an avid reader. Books, whether I'm reading or writing them, make up a huge part of my life and I wouldn't have it any other way.

www.ingramcontent.com/pod-product-compliance
Lightning Source LLC
Chambersburg PA
CBHW021951120726
47992CB00001B/242